About the author

My name is Sara Drake. I live in Bedford with my family and pets. I have always loved writing stories and have a wild imagination.

I have written another novel which has been published, called *Quest for Eden*. I also write poems in my spare time.

I loved to read as a child and my favourite writer as a kid was Dick King-Smith. My favourite author now as an adult is Anne Rice. I love anything supernatural or science fiction.

EMPTY SHELL

Sara Drake

EMPTY SHELL

Vanguard Press

VANGUARD PAPERBACK

© Copyright 2020
Sara Drake

A CIP catalogue record for this title is
available from the British Library.

ISBN 978 1 784655 45 7

Vanguard Press is an imprint of
Pegasus Elliot MacKenzie Publishers Ltd.
www.pegasuspublishers.com

First Published in 2020

Vanguard Press
Sheraton House Castle Park
Cambridge England

Printed & Bound in Great Britain

Dedication

I would like to dedicate this book to my six lovely children.

I would like to thank too my whole family and my friends who have always believed in me.

I would also like to acknowledge my dad and step-mum, Ann, for their help to realise my dream.

I want to thank my lovely mum and also my uncle, Graham, for always being there for me through the bad times.

To my late Granny, who gave me some inspiration for this book. Missed, but never forgotten.

Finally, I would like to acknowledge all those suffering from mental health issues. You are not alone.

Lost Chance

I got scared and lost my one and only true chance.
My soul in chaos it no longer moves in the same
direction towards our dance.
My heart has split and cannot continue to grow together
on his branch.
I hear his soft voice and his words are still able to send
my mind into a technicoloured trance.
Now my dreams won't ever flower or bloom even in the
month of March.

By Sara Drake

Chapter One

My hazel eyes flickered open. Parted window curtains allowed a small ray of golden sunshine to highlight the swarm of painted fairies on the high arched ceiling. The characters above the bed told me where I was, but I couldn't for the life of me remember how I got to be here. Trying to filter chaotic thoughts flashing through my mind, I pushed down the unicorn covered duvet. I sat up, staring around in disbelief at the small attic room, I saw that nothing had changed since my last stay over, which was years ago. I could see the beautiful white rocking horse, its long, flowing mane and tail which I loved riding as a small child. Next to it on a small table was a dollhouse, but this was not your typical run of the mill dollhouse. No, nothing was ever normal in this house. It was a perfectly carved wooden castle, filled with little fairies, elves and gnome figures. My uncle had made it for my sister Donna, and me.

Suddenly I noticed I wasn't in my PJs, I was wearing a pair of jog blue bottoms and a soft yellow baggy top. Strange… I thought to myself, but everything right now felt strange. The moment my bare toes touched the cold wood floor, I jerked them back under the cover. Leaning over the edge of the mattress, I peered underneath the white four-poster bed for my slippers but found only my black holdall. I grabbed hold of one of the handles and hauled the bag onto the bed. I unzipped it. Rats! Whoever had packed the bag forgot to include my red velvet slippers. Thick wool socks would have to suffice.

I stepped onto the floor, better I thought, but still cold. I noticed my pink robe draped over the back of the flowery chintz chair. In the midst of slipping it on, an image reflected in the cheval, tall mirror in the corner of the room captured my attention. I stared at the woman looking back at me. Could that possibly be me? My long chestnut-brown hair hung lifelessly and dark circles under my eyes accentuated the gaunt appearance of my face. The long sleeve t-shirt and faded jog bottoms hung loosely on my emaciated five foot-ten frame. Unable to accept the picture before me, I shook my head.

I walked over to it and lifted the mirror off its hook turning it to face the wall. Twisting the blue doorknob, I opened the door and walked through it. Cold began to creep through the fuzzy socks as I padded down the hallway towards the spiral staircase. The familiar creak when I stepped on the bottom tread seemed comforting.

The richness of cinnamon blending with the aroma of baking bread filled the quaint farmhouse as I walked towards the kitchen. "Gran?" Silence answered. "Gran, are you here?" The paneled door to the pantry swung open. Silver coloured hair pinned up in a bun and rosy pink cheeks, peeked out from behind it. She could easily be mistaken for Mrs. Claus, but it was really, just my lovely grandmother, Brielle Harver.

Her rich brown eyes widened. "Gemma," she said. "I thought the pills would make you sleep longer, sweetheart."

I frowned at her. "Pills? What pills? Gran? How did I even get here?"

She placed the tin of herbal tea in her hand on the table. "Don't you remember, sweetie?"

"Obviously not, Gran! One of the last things I recall is Mum yelling that she felt powerless to help me anymore." Tears begin to well in my eyes.

"Oh, my poor darling," she cooed wrapping her arms around me. "You're with old Gran now. You're going to recover from all this; that I promise." I closed my eyes and clung to Gran. How I wanted to believe she was right, but no number of pills or counseling had given me relief. Nothing could help. The love of my life was dead and nothing could ever change that.

Gran patted my arm. "I am going to make us a nice cup of chamomile tea. Now go sit yourself down in the living room. I just added more wood to the fireplace, so it should be nice and cozy in there."

I nodded, swiped at my tears and headed for the living room.

I loved this old house. Whether it was the house or Gran who made it special, this place seemed almost magical.

Although not the typical grandmother, despite what some people called her, Gran certainly wasn't a witch. Rumors probably fueled by the architecture of my second home.

With the orange bricks a red terracotta roof, arched shuttered windows and elaborately detailed white trim, it resembled a giant gingerbread house.

The farmhouse had been in our family for generations, and according to Gran, sat on a ley line. She claimed this meant electromagnet energy running underneath the foundation empowered everything within the house with spiritual and supernatural ability. She maintained the house might even be a portal to other dimensions. It puzzled me how my sensible grandmother could believe such a ridiculous concept.

In the living room, I sat in a blue armchair and propped my chilly feet on the matching footstool. Warmth from the flames roaring in the stone fireplace crept through my socks and inched up my legs. Watching the flames dancing in the fireplace, it almost seemed as if they were laughing at the miserable wreck I'd become.

Gran bustled into the room carrying a tray loaded with an antique teapot, matching cups, and a plateful of homemade chocolate biscuits. She placed the tray on the coffee table and filled two cups with steaming-hot tea. I accepted the cup she offered and thanked her. She thrust the plate of biscuits my way. "Come; have a biscuit, otherwise I'll end up eating the whole lot." She smiled. "And you know how I'm trying to watch my figure."

Gran was overly plump and always wore a red polka dot apron. I'd never known her to be otherwise. I laughed and took a biscuit.

Eyes twinkling, she nodded. "See, you've only been awake for five minutes and I already have you laughing."

How I wished laughter could erase the pain in my heart. Lost in my thoughts, the vintage phone on a table next to the sofa suddenly ringing made me flinch and spill my tea. Gran handed me a napkin before rushing to answer the phone. "Sorry, sweetie, I know that ring is loud. I'm afraid my hearing is going."

Sipping the flowery flavored tea, I tried to discern with whom she might be talking. It soon became clear it was my dad.

As usual, they were at odds. "I realize, Steven," she said, "you think I'm a raving lunatic, but you should open up your eyes and acknowledge not everything is black and white. There are many..." She paused, listening to whatever Dad was saying. She heaved a sigh. "Yes, Steven, I know you and her mother have done all you can to help her. But that time is long past, so for once, just trust me."

I puzzled what she meant while continuing to eavesdrop.

"Okay, love," Gran said. "I'll call you when she's feeling better." Shaking her head, she hung up.

Muttering something under her breath, she picked up her teacup and settled on the sofa. "Your Uncle Rob is eager to see you, he'll arrive tomorrow." She took a sip of tea. "But we will need to have a little talk at some point before he gets here."

"Okay, Gran, but I warn you I can't just snap out of this like Dad seems to think."

She set the cup aside, and leaning forward, patted my hand. "I know you can't, honey. More than anyone, I know your pain. When I lost your granddad, my world stopped spinning. Don't know what I would've done if it hadn't been for my two boys and this place." Her eyes looked at me sadly.

"I'm sorry, Gran. Wished I could have known Granddad; he sounds like he was a great guy."

Tears watered her eyes. "He would have adored you and your sister and spoiled both of you rotten... but such is the circle of life. One day, we'll all be together."

She swiped at her eyes and focused them on mine. "You finish all the tea and try and relax now, I am going to go start on your lunch. How about a nice bowl of tomato soup and some of my homemade bread?"

"Sounds perfect, Gran." I smiled.

She smiled back. "I told your father yesterday that I would be better medicine than that stinking hospital," she said as got up and left the room.

I could not disagree there. But it was still going to take a total miracle for my heartache to stop I thought closing my eyes for a moments rest.

I must have nodded off for a bit, as I was suddenly startled on hearing my name said loudly next to me. "Gemma, are you awake, darling? Your lunch is ready."

"Err... yeah I'm good," I replied still feeling half asleep. I dozily followed her into the dining room and sat down at the farmhouse style, oak table.

Gran walked back into the kitchen and returned with two hot bowls of her homemade soup. She placed hers down and mine next to me, then went back and fetched a tray of freshly baked bread buns. She placed the tray in the middle of the table.

Sitting down in a chair across from me, she grinned. "Eat up now, you're going to need all your strength for tomorrow."

I scooped up a spoonful of the delicious soup into my mouth. Staring at her, I could only wonder at what she could have meant by that comment as the warming soup hit my throat. But with the tall bookcase in the corner of the room, filled with rows of herbs and potions which I had never heard of on its shelves, I could just about imagine anything.

I managed to eat at least one and a half of the bread buns with the soup, before my stomach had felt uncomfortably full. It was more than I had eaten in days.

Gran placed our empty bowls on the bread tray and carried it out. I tried to gather my thoughts, but as much as I tried to keep them from the darkness, they were there all the same, ready to torment me. I started to gently sob, which in time turned into a pitiful cry.

Gran on hearing me rushed to my side and held me tight to her chest. I cried till I had no more tears to cry wrapping my arms around her waist tightly.

When the sobs grew less she slowly released me from her bear hug. "How about we put on a good old comedy on the TV and maybe grab a bit of shut eye?"

I nodded, even though watching anything on TV was hard to concentrate on.

We returned to the living room and I flopped back down on the sofa.

"Oh, how about Paul the Alien?" Gran said as she looked at the choices on Netflix.

"Yeah fine, Gran." I was not sure if I could keep my eyes open long enough, but I would give it a go.

It was strange to me as I laughed a little as I had not in the time since he had died. But I think I was laughing with Gran more than the movie. She had such a contagious laugh and good sense of humour.

I was right though, I didn't make it through the whole movie before I dozed off. But my dreams were only nightmares. I think I shouted Neil in my sleep, like in my dream as I suddenly awoke with a fright and wet cheeks.

I called out to Gran as she was not with me, but no answer. I looked up at the clock on the wall, it was about six p.m., I had been out for hours.

I got up and went to look for her. On the dining table was a note, I picked it up and read it out loud. It said in very neat handwriting:

Gemma, I have just gone down the street to buy us some nice fish and chips for your supper as a little treat. Won't be too long. Love Gran. x

I was still not hungry after the soup, but I would try as I rubbed my tummy.

It felt strange being alone in this house. I was not scared but I had an odd feeling of being watched. I looked at all the herbs and potions lined up on the bookcase shelves. I wondered what they were used for as I picked up one, on its label said 'Dragon's blood'. Interesting I thought to myself as I picked up another. This one was called Mugwort, I'd heard of this but only through movies. So weird, what does she use this stuff for I thought to myself.

As I began to walk back to the living room, I heard a noise, it sounded almost like footsteps running across the hard floor upstairs. It was not loud or heavy more like a child's. I stood and listened in confusion. It then stopped, and the house seemed eerie quiet and a cold chill came over me. I decided to brave it and started to climb the stairs. As I reached the fifth step, I swear I heard the laughter of a child. In all honesty, I did feel creeped out and nervous. It had sounded as if it was coming from the attic room where I was staying.

I slowly turned the blue doorknob, my heart beating fast as I began to open the door. I jumped back in shock! There in a corner of the room, I saw a little girl sitting next to the fairy castle doll house. She had long black hair done up in high pigtails with small red bows. She had what looked like Victorian clothes on maybe. She looked up at me with an almost confused look on her face. Suddenly I heard a noise downstairs and as I looked away for the briefest second, she had vanished.

My gran's voice calling me, unfroze me from still holding the doorknob tightly. I felt relived she was back as I raced down the stairs. I reached the bottom fast nearly bumping right into her. She frowned. "Gemma, you are you okay? You look scared like you've seen a ghost, honey."

"Umm… yeah about that. Is this house haunted by any chance?" I muttered, trying to speak.

She smiled. "Of course, it is, sweetheart. I have a few regulars and the odd ones just passing through. Oh, so what happened who did you see?"

"Well I guess I should have known it would be." I sighed. "Err... I heard what sounded like small footsteps and when I went up to see, in my room I swear I saw a little girl, possibly wearing Victorian clothing?"

Gran smiled. "Ah, yes that would be my little Suzy." She paused. "Sweet little thing, bless her. I have tried to get her to pass over to the other side, but she refuses to go. She said she wants to wait for me."

"Oh, I see. Well if you could tell her not to scare the living daylights out of me? I would very much appreciate it."

Gran chuckled and hugged me. "Don't worry, dear, I will have a little word with her."

I still thought to myself that it didn't really just happen. But I knew what I had seen and heard. Although it crossed my mind, that is was all in my messed-up imagination and that Gran was maybe going along with it. But I knew one thing for sure, that I would be sleeping with the small lamp on tonight.

The aroma of the fish and chips drew my attention to the carrier bag Gran held.

"Right, let's eat these before they get cold, then after I have a special story to tell you. Let's be naughty and go eat them in the living room in front of the fire." She chuckled.

I frowned. "Okay, Gran, that smell is actually making me a touch hungry."

It was way more chips than I could ever eat, and I felt like I was going to throw up after eating a half of the fish and some of the chips. Gran had polished hers all off and took all the rubbish back into the kitchen. She returned with more Chamomile tea. She bent down passing me a cup. Sitting back in her armchair putting her cup down and then with her hands resting on her tummy she looked right at me. "Right now, I need you to listen carefully as what I am going to tell you will cure you of this terrible burden in your soul. This is a secret few people know about. The whole thing may sound crazy, but you must trust I haven't gone around the bend like your father thinks I have."

I grinned. "Gran, I believe you are the only sane person in our whole family."

"You might want to reserve your judgment until I finish my story passed down by a Native American tribe.

Chapter Two

It's about a legend they have, but the story other people may know about them and what visited them is different to what's been written. For reasons they felt needed protecting."

She carried on. "Long ago, a great chief named Alo sensed a strange spirit mist enter his lodge. Alarmed, the warrior grabbed his knife, but the entity speaking in the tribe's tongue, said it was a Kachina, an ancestral spirit. The Kachina told Alo it could enter his body for a brief time and allow his soul to go to another realm. In this place, the chief would have the Kachina's natural form and rest in a realm filled with unimaginable tranquility. He would know only peace and joy. Promising his people would never suspect, the Kachina asked for permission to enter Alo's body and act according to memories it found there. With trouble on the horizon, Alo needed to be at his best to help his tribe overcome the difficulties ahead. After giving the matter serious consideration, Alo decided some time in the promised land of serenity, would hopefully refresh his mind and sharpen his senses. So that evening, the Kachina swapped bodies with the chief and he was transported to the other realm while his physical form remained behind." Gran paused for a breath.

Studying Gran, I began to fear Dad was right all along about her. "I don't understand what Native American Indians have to do with me or what I am going through?"

She gave me one of her looks. "Patience, Gemma."

I heaved a long sigh. "Okay, Gran. Sorry finish your story."

"Well, weeks passed and as promised, no one in the tribe suspected an imposter had replaced their leader. None save one of Alo's wives. He was growing older, and his stamina had diminished over time.

But now, when he lay with his youngest wife, she discovered his vigor much improved and he took her in new ways that both shocked and pleased her. It soon became obvious there were striking differences in her husband. He seemed much kinder and more spiritual. His hunting trips were more successful and his leadership over the tribe was stronger. Instead of sharing her suspicions with anyone, the young woman questioned the imposter, demanding to know the whereabouts of her real husband. The Kachina reluctantly revealed everything to her. The young woman told the Kachina that her parents had arranged her marriage and she'd never loved Alo. Tears streaming down her cheeks, she confessed having fallen in love with the Kachina, and asked him to remain as her husband and act as chief until the body he possessed died. The Kachina, despite having developed feelings for her, insisted such a thing could not be. She sternly said if he refused, she'd go to tribal elders and expose him as an imposter. In the middle of peace negotiations with a warring tribe, the Kachina knew that would cause great unrest. The Kachina agreed, but only if the real Alo consented.

"The Kachina returned to the other realm and presented the proposal to Alo. Having become accustomed to such a tranquil life, the chief readily agreed the Kachina could possess his earthly body until it neared death. Then Alo would reenter his shell and pass over to the great hunting ground.

"Over time, other Kachinas visited the tribe and soon they viewed exchanging bodies with the spirits as a blessing. But the number of body stealers became too great and tribal leaders then banned their people from inviting a Kachina into their body. Despite that, some secretly continued to swap with them."

Oh, my word, Mum and Dad were right! Gran was loony bin senile. With a forced smile, I inquired, "What happened to the Alo's young wife who fell in love with the Kachina?"

Cocking her head to the side, she thought for a moment. Then her eyes lit up. "You're right. I almost forgot the most important part of the story."

"Which is?"

"The Kachina, acting as Chief Alo, brought great peace and enlightenment to the tribe. He even fathered a child with the youngest wife."

"I still don't understand," I said as I lifted up my cup and took a much-needed sip of tea.

She gave me a sly smile. "That child was my great-great-great grandfather and your Kachina ancestor."

I suddenly spewed tea all over the chair.

"From the look on your face," Gran said, "I gather you don't believe me. You're also probably wondering of course where this is all going?"

I grabbed my napkin and dabbed at tea dribbling down my chin. "You might say that."

"What if I told you that Kachinas, as the Natives called them, really do exist?"

I took another sip of my tea, "Sounds pretty far-fetched, Gran."

"Gemma, look at me," she ordered.

I put my cup of tea down and looked deep into her serious eyes.

"Do you trust me, Gemma?"

"Yes, but…"

"Then believe me when I say not only are Kachinas real, but according to a wise old wood nymph, I can get one for you!"

My mind whirled with confusion. I knew things existed we didn't understand, but this malarkey was too much. Faced with the certainty in Gran's eyes, a tiny voice in the back of my mind urged me to play along. Obviously, Gran believed in Kachinas and not having the heart to crush her belief, I nodded. "Whatever you say, Gran."

She patted my knee and stood. "Right, but first things first."

I frowned at her. "What do you mean?"

"It means we'll wait for your uncle to turn up, as he said he'd be here today instead."

I watched her hurry out of the room, I shook my head. If Dad or Mum had heard her babbling about strange spirits and wood nymphs, they'd be phoning a psychiatrist for her instead.

Still feeling quite sleepy from whatever pills I'd taken or been given, I relaxed in the chair and closed my eyes. My thoughts drifted back to my last birthday, nearly twelve months ago. Instead of being a joyous occasion, it had torn my life apart.

On the way to my birthday party, Neil, my boyfriend of two years, and Louise, his sister, who happened to be my best mate, were in a car crash on the way to my party. A drunk driver had run a stop light and ploughed into Neil's car. Louise died at the scene. Neil, critically injured was rushed to the hospital by ambulance. The doctors did everything they could, but warned it was only a matter of hours before Neil would die.

I sat by Neil's bed all night, holding his hand and praying for a miracle. Watching him slip away, the injustice of it all ripped through my heart.

Six feet tall with spiky blonde hair and blue eyes, Neil had been a handsome guy with a cheeky, dimpled grin. Part of our national track team, he was looking forward to the Olympics in London next year. He'd already won an impressive array of medals and trophies that he displayed on a shelf in his bedroom. He was the fastest athlete that I'd ever seen, but that didn't compare to his funny and kind personality. He had what I described as a happy vibe about him. He often had me in stitches with his funky chicken dance while wearing a pair of his grandmother's knickers on his head. The day before my party, talking to me by phone, he threatened to do the chicken dance if he won a medal at the games. Laughing, I told him if the chicken dance caught on and became an Olympic event, he'd get the gold, although unsure his gran would appreciate her underwear being seen in public.

Chapter Three

Of the pair, Louise was the more sensible one, and quite the opposite to her brother. A touch on the short side, she was pretty with long blonde curls and brown eyes. When it rained, much to her loathing, her hair turned into a fizzled mess and she'd beg me to help sort it out. I'd spend hours straightening it until it flowed down her back like smooth silk. She was studying at the local culinary school to become a pastry chef and she made the most elaborate cakes. Aware chocolate cake was my absolute favourite she made one for my birthday party. She spent hours decorating it with small white and red roses. The cake sat on the back seat of Neil's car when the drunk driver hit them.

Neil and Louise were exceptional people. They didn't deserve to die at the hands of a drunken lout who only cared about his selfish needs.

Morning brought a glorious sunrise; one Neil would never see. Sobbing uncontrollably, I clung to my lover's lifeless body until pulled away.

The tragic incidence rattled the quaint little town of Shuttleworth. The funeral was a private one, but the town held a candlelight service to mark the loss of two people with promising futures.

Before the death of the only guy I'd ever truly loved, my life overflowed with happiness. Without my one and only best friend, Louise, to comfort me, I became depressed. Mum and Dad assured me the pain would lessen given time, but I retreated deeper into the dark shell of grief.

Mum aged forty-six, was petite with sandy, blonde hair which slightly curled just above her shoulders. She had lovely hazel coloured eyes and pretty features. She had somehow managed to drag me to a psychiatrist who prescribed an antidepressant and tranquilizers.

When they didn't help, the doctor added other medication to the mix until I felt drugged up to the eyeballs. A pill zombie operating on basic instincts, I couldn't function in the real world. Once top of my class, my studies to become a doctor spiraled downward. Classmates seemed clueless how to respond to my increasing grief. Most went out of their way to avoid interacting with me. The final blow to my psyche came when the university expelled me from the medical program. Without a daily reason to leave the house, I turned inward, almost becoming a recluse. So, it would appear that Dad, short but bulky and normally strong character, had become so distressed he'd gone along with this plan to let Gran try and heal me. I remembered his deep brown eyes so like Gran's, no longer possessed their usual sparkle. I think too he had gone balder than he was already from the stress.

A loud rattling sound startled me out of my thoughts. There was no mistaking the god-awful racket of Uncle

Rob's car as it chugged up the driveway. Along with a barely attached exhaust pipe, dents and scratches covered the dilapidated rattletrap which my uncle nicknamed Ginny. Truth told the vehicle belonged in a scrapyard. Rusty door hinges often jammed, trapping passengers inside. Several times, unable to force the front car door open, Uncle Rob crawled out the driver's side window. Embarrassed to have the pile of rust parked in our drive when Uncle Rob visited, Dad had offered countless times to buy him another car. Always sounding offended at the suggestion, Uncle Rob would reply that he had a special bond with Ginny, and there wasn't a chance in hell of him parting with his old friend. Dad would roll his eyes and shrug.

Thanks to his large chiseled chin, as a little kid I'd funnily nicknamed him Desperate Dan from the comic books. Medium height and build with greying, shoulder length brown hair, Uncle Rob was someone whose actions and appearance could be embarrassing in public. He usually wore a faded denim shirt, frayed jeans and a red-striped lumber jacket. His year-round footwear was funky leather sandals. He claimed Tibetan monks had made them and the scruffy old things brought him good luck. How he avoided losing his toes to frostbite during winter, I'd never know. Topping off his weird appearance, a large black stone dangled from a chain draped around his neck. He insisted the stone was part of a meteorite he witnessed fall out the sky. Dad would laugh saying it's just a piece of granite from Gran's garden.

If you didn't hear Uncle Rob's car coming, you'd certainly smell him when he entered the room, as more often than not, he smelled strongly of weed. He had yet to convince my dad that he used marijuana for medicinal purposes only. Worried we might get high as a kite from pot fumes inside Uncle Rob's car Dad would make him air out the vehicle before my sister and I could ride in it.

When they weren't glazed over from using marijuana, Uncle Rob had beautiful grey eyes filled with such serenity. He also often wore a huge grin on his face. For reasons I was unsure of, he believed his way of living – wearing simple clothing and using pot – made him more connected to the earth. He was what Gran would call a sensitive soul. Dad found it hard to accept anyone can be this naturally happy and carefree, so he maintained that his brother's laidback attitude was all from smoking weed.

Uncle Rob was two years older than Dad at fifty-one, but you'd think it was the other way around. They were close growing up, with Dad protecting his older brother from bullies who thought he was a weirdo. As the years passed, they took different paths. Although still fond of each other, they constantly butted heads over how the other should conduct his life.

I flinched as Uncle Rob's booming voice echoed throughout the farmhouse. Instead of saying hello like normal people, he always shouted, "Greeting, earthlings, I come in peace!"

Unable to face another lecture on how time heals all wounds, I closed my eyes and pretended to be asleep. A hand touched my shoulder. I opened my eyes.

"Hey, twiglet," Uncle Rob said with a big grin. "How's things?"

"I'm alive, I guess."

He walked around my chair and stood in front of me. "Don't fret, we're gonna sort you out. I'm glad your dad finally agreed to help us get you here."

I frowned. "What does that mean? Exactly how did I get here?"

His grin widened. "Me and your dad sorta kidnapped you."

A spark of remembrance flared. "I was in the hospital before I came here, so that's how I got here then?"

He looked sad. "Yeah, after that stunt you pulled, they wanted to keep you longer, but we had other plans."

Pieces of the puzzle began to settle into place. I pushed up the sleeves on my robe and baggy shirt and stared at the surgical gauze and tape on my wrists.

Gran walked into the room. Her brow furrowed when I touched the bandages. Emotion choked her voice. "Gemma, we love you so much. If you'll trust us, we can cure you of this terrible illness."

Tears streaming down my cheeks, I shook my head. "I want to believe you, Gran, I really do, but I don't think you or anyone else can help me. My life is over."

Gran put her arms around me and whispered soothing words of love as I sobbed. I tried to regain control, but memories locked in my mind broke free and the image of

Neil taking his last breath crushed my heart. Trapped in the past, the real world began drifting further and further away.

Gran gripped my shoulders. "Gemma, your mind is at war with itself, but you must fight back, child, you simply must!" Her stern tone parted the fog of grief surrounding me. She grabbed another tissue from the box and stuffed it into my hand. Sniffling, I dabbed my eyes.

Gran looked at Uncle Rob. "We should move on with the plan sooner rather than later."

He nodded and left the room.

My eyes were heavy, I could hardly keep them open again. I felt myself drifting off, before two strong arms lifted me from out of the chair. Uncle Rob carried me up to bed. He kissed my forehead and pulled up the duvet.

I was awoken by Gran yanking open the curtains, the sun nearly blinding me.

"Come on, Sweetie, I made you scrambled eggs, toast and a nice, hot cup of tea." She said as she pulled the duvet right off me.

Thinking to myself that I had not much choice as I was wide awake now, I followed her down the stairs, yawning. Sitting at the table, I tried to eat a piece of toast as I took tiny bites. I was not a morning person at all. And I rarely ate breakfast. But after Gran insisting, I ate a few spoonfuls of the egg and drank half the mug of tea.

Gran switched the radio on. But as with this illness, I was not in control of my emotions and just hearing about the Olympics, I could not help the tears flowing down my cheeks and splashing on the table.

"Oh, no, Beautiful, none of that now." She pulled me up from the chair. "Come, my angel, you need to purify yourself."

I resisted the tug of her hand. "What do you mean?"

She smiled. "Just that a warm bath filled with some of my lovely herbs will wash away some of your earthly burdens."

Numb with grief overcoming me again, I allowed her to lead me upstairs. While Gran ran me a bath, I rummaged through clothing stuffed in my bag. Who the hell packed this? Probably Donna. Cursing my younger sister under my breath, I discovered the only t-shirt with Mickey Mouse on it included, was one I hadn't worn in years. Who knew if it still fit? At least I found a decent pair of jeans. With fresh underwear, hairbrush and toothbrush in hand, I walked down the small hall.

I found Gran pouring bubble gel along with what looked like dried flowers into the steamy water filling the bathtub. The hot water faucet handle gave a loud squeak as she turned it off. The sound, one I'd heard many times since childhood, seemed comforting. She patted my arm. "There's shampoo in the cupboard over the sink. Shout if you need anything else."

"I will, Gran, and thank you."

She nodded and closed the door behind her.

I'd began undressing when a knock on the door made me jump. I pulled my robe back on. "Yes?"

The door creaked open and Gran stuck her head around it. "I just remembered you'll need clean dressing for… uh… for… your wounds." Avoiding eye contact, she handed me a first aid kit.

Tears welling in my eyes, I mumbled, "Thanks, Gran," and closed the door.

Guilt washed over me as I sank into the warm water. I'd put my family through so much, even Donna. Three years my junior, Donna, normally timid, had become outright defiant, arguing with Mum and Dad over every little thing. Not unheard of in a sixteen-year-old dealing with stress caused by something out of her control. Growing up, Donna always tried to emulate me, down to my hair colour. She hated her auburn hair, and secretly purchased a home dye kit. Instead of turning her hair rich brown like mine, the cheap dye job made her hair an interesting green colour. Her shrieks of horror had brought the house down and sent Mum into a blind panic to restore Donna's natural hair colour.

Feeling unworthy of a luxurious healing bath, I finished quickly, stepped from the tub and wrapped a towel around me. The t-shirt fit, but the jeans were baggy, highlighting the bony projections of my hips. Trying to avoid looking at my reflection in the mirror, I ran the brush through my hair and secured it in a ponytail with a pink scrunchie. In my room, I lay down on the bed and stared at painted fairies on the ceiling. As a small child, I believed their magic dust could transport me anywhere. How I wished they could send me back to the time when life made sense. The door opening shattered my thoughts.

"Oh, good you're dressed," Gran said, "but where are your shoes?"

Sitting up, I stared at my bare feet.

Gran muttered, "Could swear I put them next to the rocking horse last night." She chuckled. "Those damn fairies always love moving stuff about."

A quick search of the room didn't turn up a single shoe. Gran, her head cocked to one side, then suggested she might have put them by the coat rack in the foyer. Coats burdened the rack, but not a single shoe lay at its feet. Gran put her hands on her hips and bellowed, "Okay, stop piss balling about you fairies. We don't have time for games!" She grabbed my blue denim jacket and passed it to me.

Smiling at Gran's silly attempt to amuse me, I conducted another search of the foyer. A shadowy object captured my attention. Kneeling, I found my shoes cuddled up to one of the elaborate feet on the antique coat rack. I pulled out the shoes and stared at Gran. "Didn't I just look underneath the coat rack?"

She heaved a sigh. "It's those bloody fairies!" Staring at the shoes, she shouted, "All right, you wicked imps; if you want me to leave out your favourite cookies tonight, you best mind your manners."

I put on my jacket and slipped my feet into the shoes. I thought to myself I must be truly insane to trust my welfare to Gran and my hippy uncle.

Gran put on her red, wool coat, and thrust my army style fleece at me. "Wait here, Gemma, I'll see if your uncle managed to get the car running. Sometimes it takes prayers and a bit of magic to get it started."

Now that I could believe, I thought to myself.

Too restless to stand still, I wandered into the living room. I glanced up at the large mirror hanging over the fireplace. A brown finishing nail sticking out of its gilded frame caught my attention. For some reason, I couldn't take my eyes off the tiny spike. Something about it fascinated me, perhaps because its simplicity stood in sharp contrast to the elaborate frame. I walked closer and standing on tiptoe, stretched out my arm. As I started to touch it, Gran shouted from the foyer, "Okay, the car is purring like a kitten... so we're... Gemma, where are you?"

I hurried back to the living room. "Where are we going?"

"To find your salvation, my darling."

I rolled my eyes. "Exactly where does salvation live?"

She opened the front door. "An adorable spot in the woods, about ten miles from here."

I mumbled, "Figured it'd be something like that."

Gran frowned. "What did you say?"

"Nothing, Gran." Rushing past her, I told her, "Well, come on; let's get it over with."

In the car, I watched the old house fading in the distance. Although nearly spring, snow had fallen this morning, even though it was March, turning the place into Santa's grotto. Draped in sparkling white Gran's garden appeared almost magical. A deceptive picture, confirmed when the car skidded, requiring Uncle Rob to fight the steering wheel. He narrowly avoided ending up in a ditch and I breathed a sigh of relief. Devon's county council focused on main highways and streets, they didn't grit country roads most of the time. I thought about how Gran's house was the only house in the area that would always have maybe about three inches of purest snow every single year. It was a good job that Gran had no neighbours to see this and a six-foot wooden fence all around it. Otherwise it would have attracted some unwanted attention. It was the one thing that really bugged my poor dad. He tried hard over the years to come up with a scientific reason for it but had finally given up.

Chapter Four

The car slowed. I wiped off the steamed-up window with
the end of my sleeve and found we'd turned off the main
road. The car bounced crazily along the rutted dirt road.
We were deep into the forest when it sputtered to a halt.
Uncle Rob got out and helped Gran from the car. I opened
my door and slid out. I tripped over a snow-covered rut
and lost my footing. Uncle Rob grabbing my arm
prevented me from landing on my backside. I gingerly
followed Gran and Uncle Rob around undergrowth and
into a glen. The clearing was free of snow and bluebells
peeked through the carpet of leaves under my feet.
Puzzled, I looked around. Aha… Clearly the overhead
dense canopy of evergreens acted like a natural
greenhouse. Birds sheltering in the protected circle filled
the air with a chorus of music. A grey squirrel, flicking
its tail, chided us for intruding on its sanctuary. Suddenly
the birds took flight and the squirrel scampered through
nearby undergrowth. An eerie silence settled over the
glen and grew, sending a chill down my spine.

Gran nudged me. "I know one is around here
someplace."

"What?" I asked her.

Uncle Rob glared at me. "Shh!"

Gran, looking around the clearing, frowned. "It's not easy to find them." After a moment, she pointed to the base of a chestnut tree twisted with age. "Ah, there's a fairy ring," she chirped. Near the old tree, a ring of wild mushrooms poked through the leaves. She looked at Uncle Rob. He nodded.

Gran motioned for me to join her. "I need you to put complete faith in everything I tell you to do, okay?"

Wondering what I'd gotten myself into, I nibbled on my lip.

"Gemma, did you hear me?"

"Yes, Gran."

She put her hand in her coat pocket and pulled out a crystal attached to an ornate sterling silver chain. "Open your hand, sweetie."

I did as I was told, and she placed the crystal in my palm.

"According to the legend, this crystal originated in a highly developed spiritual civilization that existed over twelve thousand years ago. Now look carefully at it; you see how clear the stone is?"

I nodded.

"Remember what I told you about trusting me?"

"Uh-huh."

"You must have trust for the crystal to protect you."

"What do you mean?"

"Wood nymphs who live near the fairy ring told me the crystal will glow in the presence of a Kachina. Hopefully you're about to meet one and it will agree to swap bodies with you, allowing a brief reprieve for the mental torture you're under." Clutching my arm, she stared into my eyes. "If the crystal glows yellow, it means you can switch bodies with the Kachina safely. But, and I say this with great warning, if the stone glows blue, do not under any circumstances, agree to the swap."

"Why?"

Concern crinkled the corner of her eyes. "A blue glow means the Kachina is a Soul stealer. It will swap bodies with you, but never allow you to reclaim your earthly form. You will be trapped in the other realm for eternity."

I didn't believe anything would actually happen, but my life was miserable, so living in a different realm didn't strike me as a bad thing.

"Gemma, are you listening?" As she shook my shoulder, concern framed her words.

"I'm listening, Gran."

"When you want to reclaim your body, hold the crystal against your heart and say, I reclaim all that is mine." The crystal will glow yellow, forcing the Kachina to return and surrender your earthly form." She lovingly brushed a lock of hair off my face. "Take as long as needed to recuperate, my darling, and do not worry about leaving this realm behind. Everything will be fine here. Okay?"

I nodded.

Gran took the crystal necklace from my hand and placed it around my neck. "Stand inside the fairy ring."

I glanced at Uncle Rob. He gestured towards the ring of mushrooms. I sighed and stepped into the so-called fairy ring. This is going to be embarrassing, I thought to myself.

"Now hold onto the crystal," Gran said. "Close your eyes and repeat after me: Kachina, I ask for a swap. Walk into my body and relieve my suffering until I ask to return to my earthly form."

Feeling stupid, I clasped the crystal to my bosom, and closing my eyes repeated the chant.

A cold breeze rose and swirled around me.

Upon opening my eyes, a brilliant golden light nearly blinded me. Squinting, I discovered I stood on an expansive, tropical warm beach covered with multi-colored sand that sparkled like gems. Twin moons hung in a cloudless, bright purple sky stretched over an ocean that shimmered like quicksilver. In the distance, I saw something golden coloured floating in my direction. Shading my eyes, I watched as it glided effortlessly across the beautiful sand. An almost transparent opalescent flame outlined its form, growing increasingly brighter. It possessed a female humanoid upper body, but a wispy blue ghost-like tail replaced where legs should be, one that swished back and forth as it moved closer. The perfection of the bald creature's feminine face reminded me of sculptures created by the high Renaissance master, Michelangelo, but without nostrils.

The creature stared at me with overly large almond-shaped eyes, which sparkled like blue Topaz crystals. "Hello, I am called Valla. If you wish, I'm willing to ease your suffering by inhabiting your body and living in your world. Meanwhile, you can refresh your mind and body by assuming my identity, for my realm free of stress."

Her small toothless mouth didn't move, and yet, I distinctly heard every word. Thinking I must be dreaming, I backed away.

She offered her hand. "Don't be afraid. I mean you no harm."

I took another step backwards. Just thinking the words not knowing if I could speak with my mouth or mind, I thought the words. "But… I… uh…"

A slight smile tugged at the corners of her mouth. "After all, you requested my help, did you not?"

A valid point, but still, I hesitated to accept it. I clasped my hand over the crystal Gran gave me and found much to my relief it was alive with sunny yellow color. So, Valla wasn't a soul reaper or whatever they were called. Not knowing what to expect nerves made my voice tremble. "Okay I accept your gracious offer."

"As you wish," Valla told me. "First though, with your permission I must have access to all the memories stored inside your mind. Otherwise, people will detect I'm not actually you." She touched my head. I flinched. "No need for alarm," she told me. "The only discomfort caused by the transfer is minor pressure."

A bitter wind pierced my forehead and memories stormed through my mind, including ones of Neil and Louise. Suddenly, the mental storm ceased, and serenity seized me.

"Please remove your crystal," Valla said. "You will need to wear it while you are in my body."

I unclipped it and passed it to her.

"Now close your eyes, Gemma."

I did as she instructed. I felt a hand touch my chest and something akin to an electric shock shuddered through my body. A weird tugging sensation followed. All at once, a churning began. Deathly cold gripped my body and a dark tunnel sucked me into its mouth. Feeling weightless, I tumbled through an undulating darkness that rose and fell with the speed of a rollercoaster. Abruptly I tumbled into brilliant light, quickly realizing I was floating in the air. I looked down at the rainbow beach below. I didn't see Valla or anyone else. Wondering if I could truly fly, I spread my arms and tried to maneuver my body. Nothing happened. I seemed glued in place. Holy hell! Would I stay suspended until time to return to my earthly body? Then I noticed something even more alarming. My once normal hands were yellow and glowed with the intensity of a florescent bug light.

I decided to give flying another try. Instead of soaring with birdlike grace, I tumbled through the air and plunged downward. Screaming at the top of my lungs, I squeezed my eyes shut against the sight of the ground rushing up to meet me. Instead of crashing into the beach, the downward spiral slowed, and I floated gently to the ground.

Astonished and certain Valla had exercised some magical power I glanced around, and found I was alone. The sound of the sea caught my attention. The silver waves hitting the sand made a metallic tinkling sound like to a wind chime dancing in the air. I floated closer to the water, but something like a force field or something sent me flying backwards and my head hit the ground, blurring my vision. I tried to focus my eyes, but darkness descended.

When I regained consciousness, I felt odd, as if I'd been drugged. A greyish haze hovered over where I lay. A sudden sense of dread made me float up. A group of glowing creatures like Valla floated around me.

One with a masculine face offered me his hand. "Welcome. My name is Relik. You just arrived from the Beach of Transition, yes?" Like Valla, he communicated by transference.

I decided to ty the same back. "I'm called Gemma, and if you mean the colourful beach, then yes, I have."

He nodded. The others also all nodded. Wow! The whole group knew what I was thinking! How in hell could I keep them from knowing something I wanted to keep private?

Please don't worry," Relik said. "I regret you find our telepathic ability disturbing, but I assure you that our culture honours individual privacy. From when you say we will never invade your mind unless invited; to do so would be counterproductive to your healing process."

He offered his hand again. "I am to be your guide while you're in Sanctuary," he now said using his mouth to speak. So, I can talk with my mouth too, I thought to myself how strange.

I hesitated for a moment before placing my hand in his. To my surprise, it felt solid and humanlike.

"Err very nice to meet you and yeah if could all not be in my head that be great." I spoke out loud.

He smiled. "It's my pleasure, and of course we will talk like humans do from now on."

The other creatures began swishing their tails and disappeared into the mist surrounding where I floated.

"Please allow me to acquaint you with our world. Time in this realm is different; a week here represents just a day back in your world. Day never fades in this dimension, so we do not have what you call night time."

"You don't sleep?"

He smiled. "We do, but only when we want to dream, or are needing to save stored energy. But the transferred souls who reside within our bodies, do need sleep as part of your healing process and something you will soon experience. We also have no need for food, but we do need to recharge if you like, which is another thing you will find out in due time. We do however need to drink fluids from the underground river. But this is stored differently to humans, we only need to about every half year or so to you. And we use all of it with no waste left over."

His tone was calm, almost hypnotic. For some unfathomable reason, I felt safe in his presence, an unfamiliar sensation. I couldn't remember the last time I'd trusted a stranger this quickly.

"I'm pleased you feel at ease with me," he suddenly said, smiling.

Reminded he could read my thoughts, I did my best to shut my mind down. "Hey! You said no more mind reading."

"I am so sorry, it's difficult not to with you being in a Kachina body and I have only been a guide a few times."

I looked down at my new body; it was kind of freaky but cool at the same time. "Okay, well I will let you off if you do happen to read my thoughts. I guess it must be a tough habit to break."

He smiled. "Come," he told me. "Transformation can be stressful for humans. I suggest you visit the Lake of Dreams. It will help you adjust to inhabiting Valla's body."

Before I could respond, he tugged on my hand and we went sailing through the air. In a blink of an eye, I found myself floating on a lake comprised of bubbles the size of pebbles and glittered like red rubies. Cautiously, I pushed my hands underneath the surface. Shocked by their firm and yet squishy texture, I jerked my arms back up to the surface.

Odd music captured my attention. In the distance, large trees with silvery-blue leaves and bright yellow trunks edged the shoreline. In their midst rose a waterfall of the same ruby bubbles, which created a musical sound as it streamed into the lake. The tune shivered across the water's surface and flowed through my body. A strange sense of peace filled me. Other beings floated past me, smiling and wished me peaceful dreams. Suddenly some force pulled me underneath the water. Somehow, I didn't panic. In fact, the deeper I sank, the more relaxed I felt. Swaddled in heavenly bliss, I surrendered to sleep filled with incredible dreams.

Upon awakening, the ruby coloured water immediately pushed me to the surface. I saw Relik floating above where I lay. He held out a hand and I placed mine in his.

He smiled. "Did you rest peacefully?"

"I did."

"Then you are refreshed?"

"Very much so; is everything that happens here so wonderful?"

Some emotion I couldn't read clouded his eyes. "As long as you don't wander into the Detention pit."

"The Detention pit?"

Drifting away from me, he gestured for me to follow. "Come, I will show you."

The tail of Valla's body fluttered underneath me. I followed him. "Relik, isn't this place a Haven?"

"It is, but dark forces are everywhere, Gemma, even here."

"What do you mean?"

He turned and looked at me, his countenance grave. "What do you know about soul stealers?"

"Umm... not much; I've heard some Kachina will swap bodies and never give it back to the rightful owner."

"Yes, but to prevent dying itself the stealer must release its hold on its host a few seconds before death. Then the soul thief is automatically transported back here."

"How sad for the rightful owner. What happens to the stealer when it returns to this realm?"

"Come, I'll show you." A few moments later, I saw two massive stone pillars engraved with strange alien like symbols. An enormous crater carved in the earth lay between the columns. As we grew closer, a chill rose up into the air and an eerie feeling wrapped around me. Suddenly, a grinding noise pierced the silence, accompanied by horrible screeching. I peered down at the crevice below. From its white spinning vortex, wispy golden hands and arms desperately stretched upward, beckoning me to come closer. I felt myself drifting downward.

"No closer, Gemma," Relik said, jerking me to his side. "It's not safe!"

Taken aback by his tone, I stared at him. "What is this place?"

"It's a holding chamber to prevent stealers from contacting humans. Unfortunately, some manage to escape. If not for your protective amulet, they would have drawn you into their prison."

"I've already swapped bodies with a Kachina, so how could a stealer pose a danger to me?"

"Somehow, stealers have developed the ability to overthrow a Kachina who possesses a human soul."

"I don't understand."

"Although you no longer inhabit your earthly body, an invisible thread connects it to your mind. Stealers desperate to escape this pit sense that psychic connection. They would overthrow Valla and take over your body. Regrettably, that would mean you would be trapped here forever.

"What would happen to Valla?" I replied shocked.

"Without a host body, she would wither and die."

"That's awful! How did my grandmother think I'd find peace here?"

He placed his hand on my shoulder. "You shall please believe me."

I glared at him. "I don't view being stalked by escaped soul stealers determined to take my body and murder Valla as a peaceful existence."

"My duty as your guide is to ensure your safety."

"If Valla isn't safe in my body, why should I believe you can protect me?"

"I have been endowed with powers of protection. Whenever you're in my presence, my mind shield will protect you. However, if you wander into the force field of the Detention pit without me, you will be defenseless. The stealers will immediately detect you are a human soul and try to compromise your mind."

I stared at him. If I'd known how dangerous the pact I'd made was, I would have never agreed to the swap. For all I knew a stealer might have already seized control of my body from Valla. The thought of what might be happening to my family made me nauseated.

Relik held my hand. "Please don't worry, Gemma. Your earthly body hasn't been compromised. Valla is in full control."

"How do you know?"

He smiled indulgingly. "I know."

"But—"

"Trust me, Gemma; everything is as it should be. Please, allow me to take you someplace far more pleasant." He tugged on my hand and we floated through the air.

Within seconds, I saw what looked like an immense castle glittering like diamonds in the distance. On closer examination, it appeared to have a collection of hexagon-shaped caves carved into it. They looked cold, foreboding. I resisted Relik tugging on my hand.

"This is the castle of remembrance, a place that soothes the mind."

Still, I resisted. Other Kachinas floated past us, each one wearing a smile.

"See, it's perfectly safe," Relik told me.

Chapter Five

Reluctantly, I allowed him to pull me inside one of the caves. Large crystal speleothems rose up from the cave floor, glowing different colours, Some Kachinas were touching them.

Relik smiled and gestured me towards one of the speleothems. "Place your hand here, Gemma."

I slowly reached out and touched one of the crystals. An electric jolt surged through the centre of my body. I jerked my hand back and frowned at Relik.

"Don't be alarmed," he told me. I gingerly pressed my fingertips against the speleothem. As I did, a montage of images began to form. Some were from my childhood. Louise and I pretending we were princesses in the park. The day I bought my first guinea pig, Smudge, with the pennies I had saved. Christmases, birthday parties, and holidays spent at Gran's with my parents flashed. I watched as all of us, including my Uncle Rob ice-skated on the pond, with Donna landing on her backside more than once. Tender longing threaded my heart as I watched Neil kiss me for the first time. Lying together on a beach in Devon, lit by sunset, we shared our dreams and hopes for the future. How I longed to be in his arms again.

"I am sorry, Gemma. Even pleasant memories can be painful to someone who is grieving, but we have found concentrating on positive things is useful in the healing process."

I blinked away the tears blurring my vision. "My counselor told me the same thing, but no matter how hard I tried I couldn't conjure up good memories on my own."

"That problem doesn't exist here. The crystals always evoke memories of pleasant things, and a mind and soul's connection with one of the crystals can transport you into the past."

I frowned at him. "You can't be serious?"

"Oh, but I am," he answered with a slight smile. "The crystal speleothems inside these caves can act as a conductor that allows you to relive an event in your life as if it were happening now."

"Can the past be —"

"No, I am sorry," he interrupted. "You can't change anything it's just a replayed memory that you are placed into. It will be brief too, I will call out to you when you should return.

My heart sank. I stared at the glowing speleothem in front of me. Could I endure being with Neil again, only to have him snatched out of my life once more?

"Even if the event you chose to revisit won't technically be real," Relik told me, "it might help resolve unsettled issues."

My longing to see Neil once more made the decision. "Tell me how to make this mind and soul connection."

"Place your hand back on the speleothem and concentrate on the event you want to revisit and imagine yourself there."

I choose the day Neil and I spent at the beach and laid my hand on the crystal. It began to glow. Closing my eyes, I focused my thoughts on Neil. I felt myself drifting through space. In a flash, I was lying on the beach beside Neil. He smiled and pulled me into his arms. The feeling of being back with him filled me with unspeakable happiness. His eyes twinkled and then he kissed me full on the lips. Bliss was the only real way I could fully explain it. After a few moments, I heard Relik calling my name. As I watched Neil fade away, sadness swirled through me like an emotional tornado, wrecking my heart and broken soul.

Relik held me to him. "I am so sorry, Gemma, but to heal, it's essential to grieve. Unleash your emotions... Be sad... Be mad, but cling to the good times. Only then will you come to terms with your loss. So, don't hold back!"

Racked by refreshed memories, I sobbed hysterically, then shouting I cursed God, fate and the drunk driver who killed my Neil and Louise. I wished the driver of the car had never been born or that he died in the accident too. I cried out, "Why is God so cruel to take them away from me and their family? What was the sense in it or anything?" Surprised I could even cry tears in this body I wiped the tears from my eyes.

Relik encouraged me to keep on going.

I screamed. "It's not fair, why could I have not been in the car and died with them also. Why is it that good people are the ones to die, yet the bad people who deserve to die they get to keep on living? Where is the justice!"

When the emotional storm finally waned, Relik raised my chin until our eyes met. He then gently pulled me closer and I lent my head down on his shoulder. More tears dripped down my face.

"Crying is a good form of release, Gemma," he said as he broke free from me.

I looked at him and stared in wonder. What were Kachinas? Did they only solve one purpose and was that to be shells for souls? In that moment nothing made sense at all. The body I was in could cry tears, but why? Here in Sanctuary it would seem there was nothing to be upset about.

He frowned at me understanding my thoughts. "Gemma, we can cry as you have discovered. We share the same emotions as you. We are not robots! Long before the first Kachina made a swap we were just protectors of creatures from other realms. But we still felt we lacked a real purpose. The Enlightened Circle showed us the way to become swaps for Souls. Since then we have helped countless people to recover and gain peace in their lives as they should."

Staring into his beautiful blue eyes, I guessed that made some sense. Although, not sure what he meant about being protectors of creatures from other realms.

"I know you have many other questions about this place and us, so let us go to the beach and talk."

I nodded and followed him as he led the way. On the Beach of Transition, I felt much calmer.

"Relik, so there are other life forms here in Sanctuary?"

"That depends on what you mean by life forms. Although quite different to those found in your world, we have various forms of plant life. We also have refugees from other dimensions."

I felt my eyebrow rise. "What kind of refugees?"

"Would you like to see an example?" He smiled.

"Oh, yes please!"

He zipped off towards a group of trees with glowing white leaves, long drooping branches, resembling weeping willows. I followed as Relik led me underneath the drooping branches of one tree. Its bright red bark had an unusual furry texture. I touched the tree trunk and it vibrated. I shrieked and jerked my hand away.

Relik chuckled. "It won't hurt you."

Stunned, I stared at him.

Taking my hand, he placed it on the tree again. The furry bark not only vibrated, it made a purring sound similar to a cat.

"See," Relik said, "it likes you."

I stroked the bark and to my surprise, the purring noise grew louder. "You're right. This isn't like any plant life found on earth."

"These trees are natural to our realm. We call this place The Forest of Haven, but like you there are refugees from other worlds." He motioned for me to follow. Trying to avoid banging my head on some drooping tree branches, I trailed him deeper into the woods. To my surprise, the forest interior almost mirrored those in my own realm.

Relik could read my confusion. "For other species to thrive here, we have to recreate their natural environment," he told me.

Suddenly he signaled for me to keep quiet. After a moment, he whispered, "Do you hear them?"

Straining, I made out a slight huffing noise. The sound grew louder and then suddenly a herd of magical creatures burst right into the clearing. Startled, I clutched Relik's arm.

"Oh my god! Are they real or some kind of a recreation?"

He grinned. "They are real. This is their natural form, Gemma."

Incredulous at the amazing sight in front of me, I stammered, "But they are… unicorns… a whole bloody herd of them!"

"I find them most fascinating," he told me. "Don't you?"

True to descriptions found in books of antiquity, they were big white horses with flowing manes and long swishing tails. The spiral horn on their forehead glowed with a rainbow of different colours.

"Why do their horns change colour?" I whispered to Relik.

"The colour of their horn reflects their emotions."

"Where did they come from?"

"When the Circle realized that unicorns were on the brink of extinction in your world, they transported the remaining ones here, where they have multiplied."

"The circle?"

Surprise filled Relik's eyes. "The Enlightened Circle; I assumed your grandmother told you about them."

I frowned. "Not a single word."

"Okay, well I shall tell you all about the enlightened ones later." Edging nearer to the unicorns, he added, "But right now, let us see if these beautiful creatures will let us pet them."

Mimicking his movements, I moved closer to the animals and offered my hand. Most of the unicorns snorted and backed away, but a young mare slowly approached and gently nuzzled my hand. Careful not to make any sudden movement, I laughed and gently stroked her mane. After a few moments, others joined her, including a newborn foal.

I smiled at Relik. "Is it true they have magical powers?"

"Yes, their horns have healing properties. If crushed and ingested, they can even prevent natural death from ever occurring."

My eyes widened. "You mean the powder from their horn can make someone immortal?"

"Yes, the reason they were hunted by humans." He looked upset.

"It's said in folklore that they'll die if their horns are removed."

He nodded. "But unlike other animals that have become extinct because of humans' thirst for power, the dragons managed to protect enough unicorns to replenish their species here."

"Err... wait... err did you just say dragons?"

"Indeed." He smiled.

Nervously glancing around, I sputtered, "Umm… are they… err… are the dragons here also?"

He continued petting the unicorn foal. "They don't get on with the griffins, so they were transported to another dimension."

I put my hands on my cheeks. "Wow! Gran isn't a fruitcake after all."

Relik laughed loudly.

Thinking he might be making fun of me, I frowned. "What's so funny?"

"I just find your innocence so refreshing."

I glared at him. "And obviously amusing."

His smile was indulgent.

"You need some rest, Gemma."

Irritated even more, I snapped, "What I need is for you to stop treating me like a dog on a leash."

Uneasy silence hung between us on the trip back to the Lake of Dreams.

When I awoke, I realized Relik wasn't waiting for me. Panicked, I floated over to a Kachina who was passing by. "Hello, I'm sorry to bother you, but would you know where I can find my guide?"

She smiled. "What is your guide's name?"

"Relik."

"Ah yes, I believe he is in the Land of Mists."

"Could you direct me to this Land of Mists, please?"

"It is unwise to wander around on your own. You should wait for Relik to return."

Again, I had the distinct impression all my activities were being carefully managed.

Evidently reading my thoughts yet again, the Kachina told me. "We're only concerned with your welfare. Perhaps you would like to stroll through the Stone Garden Library?"

I scowled at her. "And that would be where?"

She pointed to a group of massive brown boulders. "You can't miss it."

Guarding my true thoughts, I thanked her.

"You're most welcome," she replied. "I shall inform Relik of your location when he arrives."

I drifted towards the outcropping of rocks called the Stone Garden Library. Some rocks were stacked like totem poles, while others stood on their own. Some clumped together created bizarre shapes. I found it intriguing how they moved and changed shape. One minute they could be round; the next they were twisting into elaborate shapes that boggled the imagination. Sensing a presence behind me, I turned.

"I apologize for my absence," Relik told me, "but a matter of importance required my attention."

I directed my attention back to the shape shifting rocks. "I understand." Silence hung the air again and lengthened until I finally broke it.

"I was told you were in a place that is misty or something?"

"It's called the Land of Mists," he corrected. "An unhappy place, but it doesn't compare to the Detention Pit."

Wow, another bad place; I wondered how many dark places Relik wasn't telling me about? I was beginning to think this place guarded more secrets than archives at the Vatican Library.

"There are only two, Gemma," he replied, reading my thoughts. "I assure you both are very sadly necessary."

The stones suddenly transforming into a facsimile Vatican Library tore my attention from Relik. "What the hell?"

"The stones can transform into anything you're thinking about," he told me. "What is your favourite book?"

I shook my head. "Ya got to be kidding me? Something else that can read your thoughts! Is there anything else that can?"

"No, Gemma, I promise you that nothing else can get into your mind. Please, I read often and have read almost everything of interest to me." He smiled.

I cocked my head to the side. "Oh, and what kind of books do you like?"

"I love nature books, I find it fascinating how many species of life your realm has," he replied.

"So, what about you Gemma?"

Staring at the stones, I muttered, "Where Love Remains, a novel by Katie James."

Relik gestured at the rocks. I gasped as one turned into a large book with 'Where Love Remains', scrawled across the front. "No way," I cried. "Any book I want to read can appear here?"

"Yes. When Shakespeare sought temporary refuge here, he suggested a copy of every book written should be transferred into these stones."

"My gosh, that's amazing! And wow Shakespeare came here too. But who keeps track of all the books written daily?"

He chuckled. "The librarian of course silly."

Feeling foolish, I frowned at him. "And exactly who is this librarian?"

"Sorry," with a cheeky smirk, "I keep forgetting how naive you are. The librarian is a type of wood nymph from your realm who travels back and forth daily. Paper is made from wood pulp and she can speak to trees, so all she needs is to place her hand on a book and the data is transferred here."

"Bet she really hates Kindle books," I mused.

He smiled. "She has an army of printers at her disposal who transfer electronic books to paper."

Watching a rock transforming into the shape of an E-Reader, I whispered sarcastically, "Oh, how nice. How do you turn the pages though?"

"The stone just does it automatically, changing into the next page as you read it."

"I see." I looked directly at Relik. "So, are you going to show me this Land of Mists or not?"

"Sure, if you insist."

Chapter Six

Again, we glided along, I then noticed the air growing thicker, charged with a strange energy. On the horizon, stood a laser looking fence surrounded a wide expanse of swirling grey mist. Relik abruptly stopped and grabbed my arm.

Squinting against the glare emitted by crisscrossing lasers, I asked, "Another prison?"

"One created by uncertainty."

Annoyed by his lack of openness, I snapped, "That's a bit cryptic. Despite what you may think, I'm not a child."

"Perhaps not, but at this moment you're acting like one."

I began retracing our path. "Never mind! I have no interest in this place. In fact, I'm fast losing interest in Sanctuary and everyone who lives here."

Catching up with me, he said, "Gemma, don't be so stubborn."

"Then stop acting so bloody superior!"

"I'm sorry if I appear so. Any hesitation on my part is due to concern over your welfare. I don't want negative things here to detrimentally affect your healing process."

"Then why bring me here?"

"Because the deal you've made comes with risks… one some visitors…" Eyes clouded with thought, his voice trailed off.

"Risks? Gran only warned me of Soul Stealers."

"Humanoids know little about other realms."

"Must you always speak in riddles? Just spit it out! What is the laser fence guarding?"

He sighed. "On the surface a swap seems a simple agreement, but there are hidden traps. Once a visitor finds healing, they resume their lives. Unfortunately, some visitors refuse to leave Sanctuary, trapping the Kachina within their earthly body. In an effort to convince them to return home, we put the resistors in the Land of Mists."

Alarmed, I glared at him. "Exactly how do you convince them?"

Studying me, he shook his head. "You are different than other earthlings I have met."

I met his gaze straight on. "How so?"

"Most are so desperate to escape their problems they meekly accept whatever they encounter in Sanctuary."

"I don't meekly accept anything," I retorted.

Puzzlement filled his face. "Why do you honor the attitude responsible for creating so much turmoil within your soul?"

"I don't know what you mean?"

"Oh, but you do. Failing to accept what can't be undone caused you so much pain you resorted to desperate means."

Tears stinging my eyes, I turned away.

He gently touched my shoulder. "Gemma—"

I whirled toward him. "Well done, Relik!"

Surprise carved his features. "Now I am the one who doesn't understand."

"You used my emotional vulnerability to avoid answering what happens to visitors imprisoned from my realm in the Land of Mists."

"I regret that my words have really upset you, but questioning things beyond your understanding is not productive to your healing."

Growing angrier by the minute, I shouted, "Are you inferring I'm too stupid to understand what happens inside the fence?"

He heaved a sigh. "Not my intent, Gemma, I assure you visitors held in the Land of Mists aren't mistreated. The fence simply prevents them from accessing other regions of Sanctuary. Forced isolation persuades most to reclaim their bodies. Others refuse, dooming the Kachina who inhabits their unwanted body." His face was tainted with a deep sadness, he guided me away from the Land of Mists.

Looking over my shoulder at the laser fence, I had the distinct strange feeling that there was an untold connection between Relik and the Land of Mists. But unexpectedly something streaking across the sky captured my attention. "Oh, my god is that a dove?"

"Not exactly."

As the creature flew closer, shock shuddered through my body. The bird possessed wings, but it suddenly morphed and possessed a somewhat humanoid appearance. Staring at Relik, I spluttered, "Err... is it... uh... an angel?"

Tone grim, he said, "It's a Seraph."

"You don't look pleased. I thought Seraphs or angels were good?"

"They are, but this Seraph is here to guide a Kachina to someone suffering horrendous abuse. The victim is usually a child."

Shock made my voice tremble. "Are you saying at this very moment a child is being tortured or murdered?"

He nodded. "In such cases, time is of the essence, so the Seraph foregoes the usual ritual and the angel rushes back here and finds a Kachina to possess the sufferer's body where it will endure the pain. And without the victim's consent, it gathers the person's soul into its own body."

Watching the bird like creature flying toward us, I asked, "Does this Seraphim want you to go to the sufferer?"

"No, only an elder is strong and wise enough to endure such a traumatic event."

"What happens to the child's soul after death?"

"That I cannot answer," he told me. "Kachinas don't experience death."

"Do you get ill or grow old?"

"No."

"You're immortal?"

"We are in this realm, like I was saying a Kachina trapped in an earthly body at the time of death will die also."

I watched the Seraph bank left and speed towards a huge blue mountain in the distance. Thinking of the child filled my heart with sadness. My pain paled when compared to the horror some child was enduring. A single tear ran down my cheek.

"Self-condemnation isn't helpful, Gemma. Plus, you must think of only yourself while you're here."

"But—"

"What is happening to that child is beyond your control. However, your loved ones are praying for your recovery. Here we can offer the healing you need... if you cooperate."

I felt annoyed. "I suppose your definition of cooperate is going along with whatever I'm told?"

He heaved a sigh, first time I had seen him do it. "Gemma, underneath your facade is a very special quality struggling to break free. I believe if you can fight through your pain you can achieve so much. You're capable of doing much more good in your world than you yourself believe. You have something extra special about you, Gemma. I can feel it under the surface of your dark suffering. It wants to break free and is trying hard to emerge." He smiled.

Suddenly, I felt uncomfortable under his gaze. I looked away, but he took hold of my hand.

"First, no matter how difficult, you must fight through this."

Tears flowing down my cheek, I shook my head. "The past refuses to release me."

"A glimpse into the future might loosen the grip grief has on your soul." He gently wiped away tears easing down my cheeks. "Come," he told me, tugging on my hand.

In a few minutes, we landed on the mountain the Seraphim did. A myriad of tunnels resembling giant rabbit burrows pierced the mountain's face. Kachinas were entering some of the channels.

A feeling of dread was creeping up my spine, I looked at Relik. "What are the tunnels?"

"They are gates to the future where one can glimpse what life might hold in store. If you truly desire to overcome the past, Gemma, choose a tunnel."

I stared at the dark openings in the mountain. "Does it make a difference which one I pick?"

"No, the result will always be the same."

Never a fan of confined spaces, I asked, "Can you come with me?"

"I'm not permitted to accompany you or influence your choice, but I can tell you whatever tunnel you choose will have two branches. One tunnel will reveal what may happen if you stay mired in turmoil. The other one shows your potential if your life is well-lived."

I mumbled, "Sounds like a Christmas Carol by Charles Dickens."

Confusion written on his face, he frowned. "I'm not familiar with the reference you use."

"I didn't expect you to be."

"My understanding isn't necessary," he said, nudging me forward. "Now do choose a passageway, please."

After thinking it over, I decided what the hell and entered the nearest passage. A cold wind greeted me, stirring up a sense of foreboding. I cast a glance back at Relik. He smiled and said, "I'll be waiting for you, I promise."

Somewhat reassured, I moved deeper into the tunnel. Abruptly, some force sucked me downward, into ever-increasing darkness.

As I plummeted, images began forming in my mind. The first one was a joyous celebration with my parents, also my gran, Uncle Rob and Donna. They were congratulating me on becoming a student doctor in a London hospital. Another image took its place, one depicting a man and woman thanking me for saving their child's life. The picture faded, followed by an image of me holding a tiny newborn. A man whose features I couldn't make out well was kissing my forehead. Was he my husband and did I hold his child?

Another vision gathered, one where I saw the same fussy featured man watching me helping two small children decorating a Christmas tree. One, a boy, had curly brown hair. The other was a girl with long blonde hair tied up in pigtails. Mum and Dad sat on a sofa laughing at Donna, who was trying to stop a toddler from ripping open presents waiting to be put under the tree. A pleasant looking man, clearly the child's father, helped her enclose the little girl who was the spitting image of Donna.

Drawn deeper into the tunnel, I saw an older version of myself sitting on a garden swing. The air was rich with the fragrance of flowers. The elderly man sitting next to me leaned over and kissed me, then handed me a glass of red wine. I smiled at him my eyes shining.

Suddenly, a doorway appeared, and something pushed me through the opening.

I saw a woman sprawled across a disheveled bed. An empty pill bottle lay beside her. Ragged sobs racked the man kneeling by the bed. Moaning, "Why," he gently brushed tangled hair from off the woman's emaciated face. I gasped. The body on the bed was my own! Misery filled my father's eyes as he kissed my lifeless face. The scene morphed. My parents and sister stood by a fresh grave. Dad seemed in shock. Tears streaming down their faces, Mum and Donna were clinging to each. Uncle Rob supported Gran who appeared on the verge of collapse. With a great cry, Mum tore free of Donna and threw herself down on my grave. I screamed, "Mum, I'm all right! Gran, Dad, I'm still alive," but they couldn't hear me.

Again, I swirled through darkness, landing in a dimly lit room. Dad, his hair grey and reeking of alcohol, sat in a faded armchair. I watched as he pushed himself upright, stumbled across the room and picked up a whiskey bottle lying on the floor. Finding the bottle dry, he threw it against the wall, spraying the room with broken glass. Where was Mum? There wasn't any sign of her living in the rundown sleep-in apartment. No women's clothes hung in the closet with a single door dangling from only one hinge.

Suddenly, I was in a hospital emergency room. I watched horrified as doctors tried to restart my sister's heart. Horrified, I heard the doctor say it was useless and announce the time of death. Turning to a nurse, he said, "We didn't have a chance against the drugs in her system."

The nurse patted his shoulder. "You did everything possible. Needle marks on her arms confirmed her fate was sealed a long time ago."

In a flash, I stood in a cemetery. Donna's grave lay between mine and another one. On closer inspection, I gulped on seeing it was my mum's and she had died only a year after me.

Shrieking, "Why," repeatedly until I felt a sudden forceful pulling and then I was back outside the mountain, where Relik waited. Crying, I rushed into his open arms. "Don't fear I got you. The path to recovery is often a painful one," he whispered as he rubbed soothingly one of my arms.

I clung tighter onto him, I cried, "I want to break free of the darkness holding me prisoner... but it... it would... be betraying Neil."

"Do you think Neil wanted you to just become an empty shell, of yourself," Relik said softly. "No, he'd want you to be happy."

I nodded, but I longed for Neil... for him to be the one holding me, telling me we'd be together forever. Uncontrollable sobs shook my body, and everything turned black.

I awoke in the Lake of Dreams.

"How are you, Gemma?" Relik asked when I rose up from the water.

"What happened? How did I get here?"

"Your energy level became critically low."

"Umm I fainted?"

"I believe it's called that in your world. I transported you back to the Lake of Dreams."

"Oh okay." I smiled. "Thanks for comforting me yesterday and taking care of me."

He kind of bowed. "You are most welcome. As your guide, it's my job to protect you."

A job, that's all I am to him, I thought.

"It's also my pleasure," he swiftly told me smiling.

I scowled at him. "What happened to you trying to not read my personal thoughts? You still keep on doing it, Relik."

"I apologize for trespassing but isn't the ultimate goal of criticizing someone to improve their conduct. How can I improve mine without knowing what I'm doing wrong?"

Trying to smother a smile, I said, "You're impossible!"

A grin on his face, he offered his hand. "Speaking of pleasure, how about us indulging in some fun?"

Intrigued by what Kachinas considered fun, I laid my hand in his. He pulled me through the air toward a huge yellow dome. Pointing to the building floating in the air, he told me, "This is a recreation hall, but that is all I shall tell you for now."

"Based on your past behavior, I expected nothing else," I chided.

Although the recreation center shone brightly on the outside, the interior was devoid of much light, except for small illuminated orbs spinning through the air and other Kachinas with their own glowing outlines. The sparkling balls made cute squeaking noises as they whizzed through the air.

"What are these things, Relik?" I asked, as one orb zipped past my head.

"They're Chamalims." He laughed at the other Kachinas speeding through the air and trying to trap the balls in glowing nets. He cheered when a female Kachina caught an orb in her net. I recognized her as the one who'd directed me to the Stone Library. She laughed and waved at Relik. He returned the acknowledgment. Fetching two nets from a rack on one wall, he offered one to me. "The game is called Catching Joy and it's not an easy one."

I refused the net. "I don't understand the point of chasing and tormenting helpless creatures."

"Chamalims are extremely fast and clever little creatures who enjoy pitting their wit and speed against others. They also have healing qualities. When you manage to catch one, it rewards you by sending joy through your body. The winner of the match is whoever traps the most Chamalims." He shoved the net into my hands.

"Uh... okay... but I warn you games are not my forté."

He shouted, "Let the match begin!"

At his shout, the energized balls begin speeding faster. Unsure of rules governing the game, I followed him into a group of Kachinas intent on preventing other Kachinas from capturing their target. I tried to mimic Relik's moves, only to be promptly bowled over by a competitor. Embarrassed, I righted myself and managed to avoid a repeat incident. Irritated, I threw caution to the wind and zipped after the same orb the offending Kachina was chasing. Relik was right; it definitely wasn't easy. In addition to having to fend off and avoid opposing players, Chamalims proved worthy adversities. The tiny creatures' speed and maneuvering abilities boggled my mind. One, trying to evade an opposing player, zipped recklessly through the air — straight at my head! To protect my noggin, I jerked my net upright. The bright orb flew in my web! A feeling of immeasurable joy and happiness washed over me. Lost in the feeling, it took a few moments to realize other Kachinas were cheering my catch. On the other side of the playfield, Relik smiled and waved to me. Somehow, his smile outshone the success I felt.

Armed with his encouragement, off I went. Time stood suspended as I rushed through the air. In the end, I managed to capture four Chamalims, but Relik proved the most masterful Chamalims catcher. When he tried to return my net to the rack, I refused to release my hold on the precious web.

"Too much joy isn't necessarily a good thing," he admonished. "It can make other things seem anticlimactic. Besides, it's time to renew your energy."

"But I'm not tired."

"Excuse me, Gemma, I misspoke. You inhabit Valla's body and she needs renewal.

"I thought you said Kachinas didn't need rest."

"We don't, but our energy source needs renewal."

I gave him my net. He returned it to the rack hook and took my hand. He tugged me into the stream of other Kachinas, all headed to an enormous orange pyramid. Hieroglyphic symbols covered the exterior. An iridescent red sphere on its apex crackled with electrical energy. I tightened my grip on Relik's hand.

Chapter Seven

We got even closer up to the huge structure. I squeezed his hand again. "There is no cause for alarm. The pyramid is a storehouse, where collected energy is stored and transferred to Kachinas to sustain their life force."

"Where is this energy collected from?"

"From other dimensions, including yours."

I gasped and jerked my hand from his. "You're stealing energy from other realms!"

"No, Gemma, of course not. All life forms are interconnected, but each one has different requirements. Your realm produces energy which humans or other life forms on earth cannot access. The unused energy from your world filters into other dimensions that collect and put it to good use. Each dimension also produces its own waste matter, including energy needed by another world. The process creates a never-ending circle of energy."

"Oh," I replied a little sheepish.

The pyramid's door opened and Kachinas streamed inside.

I felt obligated to take care of Valla's body, but uncertain what it might entail, I hung back. "This transfer… is it… will it hurt?"

Relik smiled. "Surely, Gemma, you know by now I won't let anything harm you." Reluctantly, I followed him inside the strange structure.

Kachinas filled the main chamber. Some knelt around an altar in the centre, with tentacles of colourful energy from the pyramid's apex attached to their heads. After a few minutes, the rays dissipated and the Kachinas rose. Others waiting in line took their place at the altar. Although the experience didn't seem to cause them pain, I grew increasingly nervous.

Sensing my apprehension, Relik this time squeezed my hand. "I promise the transfer won't be unpleasant." Before I knew it, he motioned me to kneel on my blue tail before the altar. My mind screamed to get the hell out of there, but I did as he directed. Without warning power infiltrated my head and surged through my body, making movement impossible. Suddenly, an extreme state of well-being filled me. When released, I felt supercharged, capable of moving with the speed of light.

Relik placing his hand on my arm startled me. "The energy transferred to your body... rather Valla's body, is meant to last for a set period. Do your best to conserve it. If you deplete it before its time for the next energy burst, both yours and Valla's resistance to the Soul Stealers will be weak."

The very mention of Soul Stealers sent a shudder of impending dread through me. "I don't quite understand how, but I'll do my best to monitor Valla's energy reserve."

He turned and looked me in the eyes. "Gemma, would you be interested in a conversation with the Griffins?"

I looked at him strangely. "They can talk?"

He tried not to smile, but the corners of his mouth rose ever so slightly. "Yes, many magical creatures can." He giggled. "You're going to be in for quite a shock, as I'm guessing you don't know about the snails?"

I pulled a face. "Let me guess, they can bloody talk too?"

He started laughing. "You have had such a sheltered life, even though your family have such big ties with the Enlightened Circle."

"There you go again about the Enlightened Circle. I think I'm well overdue being in the know now. So, spill it, what's the deal on them?" I scorned.

He smiled. "Even better you can meet some who are part of it, as the Griffins are. Come on let's go and see them now." He grabbed hold of my arm and yanked me forward.

After we had been floating for what seemed like awhile, I glanced over at him. "How much further is it?"

"Not too much further. You see the volcano in the near distance to your right?" He pointed, "They live just beyond it."

"Oh okay... Umm... Is that a live volcano, does it erupt very often?" I asked as we got closer and I realized looking in awe it was probably the size of Mount Everest back home.

"It's a live volcano, but not in the sense you would understand. It gives birth to life, it gives birth to us!"

I looked at him dumbstruck. "What! That is your… Err… parent?"

He laughed, but quickly stopped on seeing my slightly pissed facial expression. "Not exactly. My parents, elders are unknown to myself. They mated and gave a little of themselves fused together into the volcano. We then grow inside the life substance till we are ready to be born. Full grown."

I smiled. "So, what, the volcano erupts and out you flow?"

"Pretty much." He grinned. "We are like a large golden egg and we then split into two beings. We always have a twin brother or sister."

My eyes widened. "Oh really, where is your twin?"

He looked away and a sad silence took hold.

"Err… Relik are you okay?"

He nodded. "Yes, sorry, it's just hard to discuss at the moment. Plus, you're not here to listen to my woes; you're here to recover from your own."

I figured he didn't want to talk about it, so decided to leave it be. But I put my hand on his shoulder for a change, and gently squeezed it. He looked at me and smiled through saddened eyes.

A noise suddenly startled us as massive wings swooped above our heads. "Relik, how are you my old mate?" said a gruff sounding voice of the magnificent creature as it landed a few feet from us.

Relik smiled at him. "Jack, it's so nice to see you, my friend."

I grinned, thinking to myself Jack is his name. Not what I would have expected for such a magical beast.

Relik laughed reading my thoughts and I grinned back.

The Griffin ruffled its feathers. Big yellow eyes stared at me. "So… who do we have here then? As I don't sense Valla."

I looked in stunned disbelief at the beauty of it. Around ten-foot-high, it had the head of a golden eagle with a large blue beak, and the body of what could only be described as a large lion, its tail swishing back and forth like a cat. It's amazing, huge lavender coloured wings were now folded down the side of its long body, all finished off by big, silver coloured talons.

"No voice little one? Are you just going to stare at me all day?" He laughed.

"Umm… Sorry kind of hard not to. I'm still in shock about the Unicorns and dragons being real; it's a lot to take in. But my name's Gemma," I squeaked.

"Well, very nice to meet you Gemma. I am Jack one of the council members of the Griffins."

I wasn't sure whether to bow, curtsy or what, as he had such a regal air about him. "It's very nice to make your acquaintance," I mumbled.

He looked at Relik. "Shall we go to the great nest?"

He nodded. "Yes, I do believe Gemma will enjoy the visit."

"Come on then, friends, I do believe we shall be in time for the blessing's daily's service."

Relik gestured for me to follow Jack.

After a brief time, we came to a gigantic, green shrubbery maze. I followed quickly behind Relik and Jack. Jack strode along just like a king. Finally, we reached what appeared to be the middle, with a huge white tree in the centre of it. In its big branches was a massive golden nest, I'd never seen one so big in all my life. But that wasn't all in the tree, suddenly I noticed around fifty or so Griffins lining the thick branches. One by one, they all began to jump down and join us beneath it.

"Relik, it's always such a pleasure to have your company," said another Griffin as it approached us.

"No, the pleasure is all mine, Rachel." He smiled.

I stared starry eyed at everything, it was just so unbelievable.

"This is Gemma; she is staying here for a while until she is ready to return home."

"Gemma, welcome to our home. We were just about to perform the blessing. You're most welcome to attend."

I smiled. "Thank you, it sounds very interesting."

Jack suddenly made a loud bird like cry and they all formed a large circle around the tree.

"Where do we go?" I asked Relik.

"We are fine here I do believe."

Relik gestured for me to look upwards. As I did, smaller Griffins poked their heads out from the sides of the nest.

"Ahh so cute," I cooed.

"Okay, I think they are nearly ready to begin."

Gradually, each Griffin in the circle opened their mouths and began to sing in an unknown language. The harmonies though were just amazing. The little ones in the nests then also joined in. I felt so uplifted listening to the magical sound, like I didn't have a single care in the world. I almost felt like I was in a trance or something. I didn't want it to ever end, but even when it did, I felt like my spirit had been refreshed.

"Beautiful wasn't it, Gemma?"

"Breathtaking." I replied smiling.

Jack walked back over to us. "We sing every day, Gemma, giving thanks and praise for everything in this realm and all the others. It also has a good effect on us, and all around us when we sing."

I nodded. "I felt it myself, thank you so much for allowing me to witness something so special."

"You are most welcome anytime, Gemma. When one of the great moons starts to get darker we get ready to sing. So please feel welcome to come here again."

I nodded smiling.

"Gemma would like some information about the Enlightened Circle, Jack. She is pretty much a newbie to just about everything, even though her grandmother is Brielle," Relik said trying not to grin.

Jack's eyes widened. "I did wonder why she was so surprised about the Unicorns." He paused, "Well, Gemma, The Enlightened Circle are a group of beings from many realms dedicated to trying to keep a balance and rules within the supernatural dimensions which exist. We try wherever possible to instill punishment or reward when needed. We are also able to give guidance and counseling. Feel free to ask me anything."

I thought for a moment. "Well, the snails come first to mind. What's their deal?" I grinned.

He laughed. "Not my favourite beings, although not as bad tempered as the Dragons. The snails you mention would be the nature sprites. Why they choose that form so long ago, nobody knows. They were not corporeal to begin with but favored taking on the snail's form in your realm." He chuckled, "I guess they must have some benefits to living like that, although I can't imagine one myself."

I shrugged my shoulders. "Umm, yeah me neither." I paused to think. "So how can you tell a nature sprite from a common snail? Ooh… bet they don't live in France, otherwise they may be made into soup."

He chuckled. "You're probably right. But Nature Sprites are extremely hard to find if they don't want to be. They are normally bigger than common snails and are a shiny silver in colour. What sets them apart, other than the fact they can talk, is they glow slightly in the dark."

"I see… And can they be in anyone's garden or just certain places?"

"They tend to be where lay-lines are as they feed on electromagnet energy."

"Oh wow, Gran claims her house is on one. So, would she be likely to have them?"

"Yes, Gemma, and your gran has knowledge of the Enlightened Circle. I would say she probably has regular conversations with them."

I rubbed my chin. "So, I could talk with them when I return home?"

He laughed. "Like I said, they are not as bad tempered as Dragons can be, but they are obnoxious at the best of times. It would depend if they felt you worthy or not."

I rolled my eyes. "Probably not then."

Relik smiled. "Don't be so harsh on yourself. I personally would deem you very worthy."

I grinned back. "Thanks, Relik."

"We should be going now, Gemma. I think another rest in the Lake would be beneficial for you?"

I nodded, smiling. "Whatever you think, Relik."

After we thanked Jack again we made off for the Lake.

Drifting along I thought about things. It did not make sense at why a Kachina would choose to remain in a human body, not when they had all this in Sanctuary to enjoy. Relik quickly answered my thoughts. "There are some experiences of the flesh, which can be quite addictive and pleasurable. Just the ability of touch how humans experience it, can be overwhelming for a Kachina. Especially if it's their first swap. Feeling the wind, rain and the sun on your skin is something you all take for granted. Eating food, taste is amazing to us. Then not forgetting physical love, that's something you are very envied for, Gemma." There was an awkward silence for a moment as we looked into each other's eyes. We slowly drifted above the golden ground.

"There is a special garden for you to visit, it has some similarities to the stone garden, I feel you will visit it often."

"Do tell me more?"

He smiled. "Don't be so impatient, I show you when we get there."

I sighed. "Okay."

Off we went in search of this garden. Soon in the distance I saw what appeared to be fields of very colourful flowers.

"This is called the feelings gardens. You will see why when we get there."

Chapter Eight

We soon reached it. I looked at the beautiful flowers, some I had never seen before; some were small, while others were taller than me like giant, purple tulips. There were rainbow coloured roses and ones that looked like sparkling gems. Everything was so vivid in colour, too vivid, I would imagine, for human eyes. Relik gestured for me to follow him. We came to a large patch of lavender type plants.

"Brush your hand gently across the top of them."

As I did they made musical notes. "Wow! That's so cool."

"Yes, it is and they can sense your mood and the tune reflects it back."

I looked up at him, feeling my eyebrows rise. "I thought you said nothing else could get into my head?"

He did his usual grin. "Umm... well they don't know what you're thinking, just feelings."

"Duh... Kind of the same, Relik. They would still be in my mind to know my feelings."

I heard the first sigh come from Relik. "You humans are such a complicated species! Or just y..."

"Oh, you were just about to say me, weren't you?" I replied feeling pissed.

He frowned. "No, but you are more closed up to your emotions than others I have been a guide for and you come across as somewhat stubborn."

I glared at him before bursting out laughing.

He looked very confused as he floated towards some rainbow coloured flowers, muttering Humans!

Still smiling, I brushed my hand lightly over the heads of the flowers as I drifted along the rows of them. To my amazement, it played a beautiful happy melody and the flowers swayed to the tune. I looked over at Relik, he looked surprised before smiling back. I think we were both expecting a sadder tune. Maybe I was taking a step forward in the right direction.

And he was right I could see myself being here often, not only beautiful music, but being round the gorgeous flowers. I listened to more as I closed my eyes and floated like I was lying on a waterbed. Time passed, I opened my eyes and stared at where Relik was. He looked beautiful, even more so than he normally did. I was really starting to enjoy my time here in Sanctuary.

"Do you see how your healing can be successful in such a peaceful place?"

Stop reading my thoughts, Relik," I joked and nodded, then thought of something. "How do the flowers and trees get water? I have not seen any sign of rain, not even a single cloud while here."

"It does rain here, once a year in your time, and in a large amount. The soil is special here, it's like a sponge it soaks it all up and is enough to last until next time."

"I guess it's purple rain from looking at the sky?"

"Ha ha. No, it's the same as your water, remember we have some living things from your realm here."

"Oh, well that does not explain the liquid, metal looking ocean."

"It's actually pure silver, we have many oceans of it. It's one of the things we send to other realms to use, yours being one of them."

"But silver is found in silver mines."

"Yes, you are right. We put the extra silver there, well not actually us in person, but the Enlightened circle take it for us."

"Oh really, who knew," I smiled. "But wait, it's in liquid."

He grinned. "It turns hard in your dimension."

"You learn something new every day." I smiled.

"Also, why when I tried to cross the ocean when I first arrived did it push me back like it did?"

"That's because you were heading towards the entrance to Sanctuary, no one can enter or leave unless doing a swap. It was put there as protection after the stealers became a problem,"

"I see, makes sense, but maybe you should have a sign put on the beach warning newbies about it."

He laughed. "Maybe you're right I put it forward to the council."

"Okay so what now? Anywhere else to visit?"

"Well yeah, one more place, it's called the Irish Massage."

"Oh… that's interesting. I think I will go to this Irish Massage." I smiled.

"First you have had a lot for now, you should go back to the lake for a while first. There is no need to rush to experience everything."

"But I am impatient." I grinned.

"I am aware of that." He chuckled.

Relik flew off. "Come on catch me if you can."

I laughed. "I'm coming." And took off after him.

We reached the lake again and I sunk down into it. I did feel a little lifted in spirits as I closed my eyes. When I exited it after a good period of time, Relik smiling took hold of my hand and we went off together. As we got closer to one of the oceans I could see something in the distance. When we reached the shore, I gasped out loud. It was a ship and a pirate ship at that! It was gently rocking in the silver sea back and forth over the waves. There were large white sails with a skull and bone symbol splashed on the front one. Cannons sticking out like they were ready to attack. It looked like a genuine, old style pirate ship. But it was perfectly preserved like it was not old at all.

"How on earth did you get a pirate ship over here?" I asked bewildered.

"Oh, it got caught up in the Bermuda Triangle. Which is another source of reaching into other dimensions. It was then passed over to us to use as the other dimension had no use for it."

"Why did they not just give it back?"

He smiled. "Because the Triangle is an enter point not an exit. The closest exit for that dimension is in the north pole. Not sure how they would explain it."

I frowned. "What happened to the crew?"

"No idea? It was a ghost ship, the beings in that dimensions looked for them but no sign."

"Oh, that's a bit spooky then. Not sure I want to go on there now."

"Yeah, but don't let that bother you I am told it's very relaxing."

"Huh… you have not been in yourself?"

"No, Kachinas are banned from going on it. Massage is forbidden to a Kachina unless it has a soul within. I believe it is because we don't have a soul, maybe it's something to do with the physical experiences of being human. As you know they are strict about Kachinas liking human ways too much and then wanting to be stealers."

"Oh, I see." I smiled. "Well okay I am ready to board captain."

"Aye aye, Gemma, well float across the water and you will be welcomed by one of the leprechauns."

I coughed loudly. "Leprechauns, you got to be bloody kidding me?"

Relik laughed. "I'm not kidding you. Also, they are part of the Enlightened circle, and reasonable pleasant members too. They will give you your massage and as payment will receive a gold coin from the vast treasure which was found on board.

I laughed. "That sounds about right."

"Okay I am going, bye see you soon," I said as I started to make my way across the sea.

"Behave yourself, I don't want to hear you have been made to walk the plank."

"Haha, very funny. I will throw the leprechauns overboard first before they will get me." I laughed back.

I suddenly had a thought. "Hey! Where is my pirate sword? You're sending me with nothing to defend myself?"

He chuckled loud. "Oh I have no worries that you can defend yourself."

I frowned back. "And what exactly do you mean by that?"

He shook his head. "Don't worry about it, just go and enjoy yourself."

I rolled my eyes at him and carried on until I reached it. I was welcomed aboard by a two-foot looking leprechaun. A female one, at least it appeared to be with boob's. She had long ginger hair and blue eyes, but her nose was rather on the large size for such a small face. I grinned as the outfit was just how they were described in Irish folklore. But it was its voice that took me by surprise. It was loud and almost grumpy, I reevaluated if it was really a girl.

"You are Gemma, I assume. Please go below desk where you will be shown to your quarters." She pointed at a yellow door.

"Yes, I am, and thank you." I smiled.

She never smiled back, just nodded and went off with a bucket and mop. I opened the door and floated down the steps. So strange, here I was on a real, old pirate ship which was now being run by little people.

Down below the ship, it was like another world. Like a fairy land, twinkling little lights lit up the dark in a magical indoor forest. Strange blue grass, and large red polka dot mushrooms, lined the floor and sides of the boat. Transparent bubbles of colours floated around me and the beautiful sound of a flute was being played by a leprechaun sitting on a large toadstool. I felt like I was in Alice in Wonderland or something.

A male looking leprechaun like the one above, walked towards where I was floating. "Welcome, Gemma, I hope Gloria was in a good mood today when she showed you down here.

"I guess so." I grinned.

"Please follow me, you're in for a treat." He smiled.

I followed him to another door. "This is amazing, is this what home is like for you?"

"Not really, you would be amazed at the beauty of our home, but best we can do. Us little folk get very homesick. We take it in turns to come to Sanctuary." He laughed. "As folklore says, we do like our gold."

I laughed back.

Inside my quarters, it was more again like a pirate ship interior. It had a small window, I looked out of it and stared at the calm silver waves hitting the side of the boat. Turning around I noticed lots of different coloured candles were on a table and a massage type bed was in the corner. I wondered how this worked as I could feel touch as a Kachina, but not in the same way as being human was. There was a knock on my door.

"Please come in."

Two female leprechauns and a male one walked in. "Hello Gemma, we are here to give you your massage. Please lay above the bed do not be concerned with the strange pulling down feeling you will get. Please trust us that nothing we do will cause you any harm," said one of the females.

I did what they said and floated just over the bed, trying not to swish back and forth my tail too much. I then felt like I was being sucked down onto the bed. My head through the hole at the top of the bed. "Okay, Gemma, we are going to connect you to your real body, through your Kachina one. It is a talent we have and why they use us here. So, to you, the massage will feel just like a human one.

"Wow! Will Valla know this?"

"Yes, she will feel something and know what is happening, but she won't feel the massage. Are you ready to begin?"

"Yes," I said allowing myself to relax. Suddenly I could smell perfumed creams and oils that I noticed next to the bed. They had lit aromatherapy candles and they smelled divine. I could smell again, just like when I was human. I was surprised how much I had missed this sense.

I then felt something slightly warm and wet on my back and hands rubbing in all different motions. They were right it was just like it would really feel. Music from a violin this time played quietly in the background. It went on for quite a while and when finished I felt the pressing down feeling lift. Then I could not smell again.

I got back up and smiled. Thank you that was great. So where do you get your gold coin from?

The male one pointed over to a door. "Take that door down to the ship's galley. There you will find a mountain of treasure. But only pick out one gold coin. We think it could be cursed or something."

"So, wait… does that mean I am like a guinea pig, taking a coin and hoping it's a good one?"

He smiled and nodded.

"Fantastic! Seriously this place is meant to be peace and harmony, yet I have to go and try to dodge a bloody curse." I shook my head. "Umm I don't suppose you even know what the curse is?"

"Nope." He chuckled hard his little belly wobbling as he did.

"Why don't you go down and get one instead," I hissed.

His eyes widened, and he rubbed his little hands together, "We can't be trusted to not take more than one coin so am banned to go down. But I would not anyway as we don't want to be cursed."

"Okay well what if I don't pay you?" I folded my arms and stared at him.

He grinned at me, but it was a creepy kind of grin. "Well… we will curse you with one of our own curses."

"So… I am pretty much screwed either way then?" I said sounding rather pissed off.

He smiled, "You are, my dearie."

I went over and yanked the door enough open that I could slip through. I floated down the many steps, until finally I came to another big red door at the bottom of them. Bloody leprechauns, I cursed under my breath. This door was much harder to open, but I finally managed it. Inside was a vast treasure so bright that it blinded me and as result I went straight bang into a pile of treasure. Coins and gems slipped down with me and from within them, a golden crown with a most beautiful large emerald in the middle. My eyes now better adjusted I held it up. I looked at the sheer beauty of it. But my thoughts were suddenly interrupted as the big pile started to move and lift. The sound almost like the growl of a bear, but worse and it rang throughout the whole ship making it rock back and forth. Oops... I think the curse has begun. Panic filled me, and I called out loudly to Relik in my mind. I dropped to the floor and looked behind me, to see a large humanoid figure forming about fifteen feet tall and made out of the coins and with gems for eyes.

"Oh, holy shit! Umm... help!"

The coin monster roared into my face, I would have peed myself if Kachinas needed to.

Suddenly, at one of the port ship windows Relik appeared. "Gemma, what did you touch? What made it start to form?"

"I don't bloody know, Relik. I fell into this huge dam pile!" I replied as I quickly floated up and down trying to avoid his large arms from catching me. Suddenly I remembered I had touched the crown. I screamed. "The crown with the large Emerald, that is what I picked up."

I looked over at the window where Relik was, but he wasn't there anymore!

Just when I thought my number was up, the door flew open and Relik quickly drew its attention from me. "Gemma, look for the crown quickly!"

The monster clumsily reached for Relik, but he hit it hard in the head shape part of it. Coins fell from it flying in all directions.

"Is everything okay down there?" shouted one of the Leprechauns.

"No, it's not!" we both loudly replied together.

I scanned around the treasure, which was still brightly shinning making it harder. From the corner of my eye I thought I saw a green colour peeking out, blinking I raced over and pulled it free. "I got it Relik, I got it!"

"Break the stone, Gemma, quickly," he shouted

"How the hell am I supposed to do that?" I cried back, watching as the coins lifted back off the floor and formed his head again.

You're much stronger as a Kachina than you realize, focus hard!"

I closed my eyes, not wanting to see us both crushed to death by coins. I focused as hard as I could. Holding the stone, I put pressure on it until it started to shatter in my hand into smaller pieces. Shocked I yelled, "It's working, it's breaking, Relik."

As I said it the coin monster fell back into a huge pile of just coins.

Relief swept over me, as I looked at my hero of the day grinning. I bent down and picked up a coin for the little bastards upstairs. Relik came over to me. "Well that was very strange to say the least."

"Ya bloody think!" I giggled, then slapped him on the arm.

He looked surprised, "Hey! What was that for?"

"Go for a nice massage with the little Irish folk, Gemma, it be so nice and relaxing, Gemma," I spat then smiled.

"Come on, let's get out of here." He grinned pointing to the now broken red door. We both started to float towards it.

"You did a good number on that door, Relik, it's just about hanging there." I laughed.

"When I believed you were in serious danger, Gemma, I would have torn this whole ship apart just to save you."

I stopped and looked at his face, he was deadly serious. I slowly gave out my hand to him, looking into his beautiful eyes. He took hold of it and held it close to him.

"Thank you, Relik, that means so much. I don't know what to say."

"No words needed, Gemma…I just read your thoughts anyway." He laughed.

"Wow, you cocky sod," I giggled.

There was a pause…I drew closer towards his face and lightly kissed his cheek. His eyes lit up as he smiled.

We rose hand in hand slowly up to the top, where three nervous looking faces were peering down at us. The male one shuffled on his feet. "Sounds like you may have set off the curse, dearie."

"Now… what in heaven's name would make you think that!" I smirked.

He put his hand out to me and I passed the golden coin over to him. But Relik suddenly took it back from him. "I don't think so, she just fought a Golem off, while you guys cowered up here. This coin belongs to her, she deserves it more. She has done you a very big favor. Now no one need worry about the curse any more, as she broke it."

The Irish deity nodded. "Yes, the lass does deserve it I agree, we are indebted to you both, so, either of you ever need a favor from the fairy folk we will be happy to help,"

We both thanked him and quickly left. I had enough of pirate ships for one day.

Chapter Nine

We floated back across the sparkling water to the beach.

Suddenly, Relik made a gasping noise. He rose fast upwards into the air as if something had startled him. "Is there something wrong, Relik?" I nervously asked.

After a few moments, he broke the silence. "I need to return back to the beach of transition. Finally, my sister Aluna is due to return. She had been trapped in a swap body for about seventy-five human years, which sadly has been much longer back here. I've been waiting patiently for this day to come."

"Can I come with you? I would love to meet her."

"No, sorry. Gemma, she could be too traumatized. Possibly to the point she may have even forgotten who and what she once was. There is also a strong chance she may not adjust back. You must promise me you will go back to the lake and rest. I will return back to you as soon as I possibly can," he told me his face looking so serious.

I nodded. "I promise, and I hope everything works out okay."

Relik took hold of my hand. "Thank you, Gemma, I really hope so too." Releasing me, he floated off only turning back once to wave to me. I waved back.

I was not sure which way the lake was so I just floated about for a while. But crazy thoughts started to creep into my mind, ones which after thinking about longer enough made me decide to go after Relik. My curiosity was getting the better of me as always. Maybe if I didn't get too close it would be okay? Although I did still feel guilty for not doing as Relik had asked me, but it was my nature to be over curious. After stopping a few Kachinas for directions to the beach, I soon found it and floated along it. In the distance, I saw what looked like a portal suddenly open with a big flash of light. A small crowd of Kachinas were just beneath it. I dared to get a little closer, just before the horrendous noise came! It was the most blood curdling noise I had ever heard. A terrible screeching, so loud it physical hurt the form I was now in, as it echoed over the beach. The group of Kachinas was surrounding something lying on the beach. A transparent sort of bubble suddenly covered over the top of them all. Inside the bubble, it looked like a fight was going on. As I got up closer, I could see a Kachina throwing itself frantically up against the side of the bubble, like it was struggling to escape. There was still the terrible noise, but it was luckily now muffled inside the bubble. The other Kachinas inside with were trying to touch the one going crazy, maybe comfort it. All of a sudden it all went eerie quiet, whatever desperately wanted out had stopped trying. I took this to be as a good sign as I floated closer to the bubble.

Something fast with an unearthly screech, burst out the bubble. It came flying straight at me and grabbed me by the neck. A terrible pain swept through me, similar to when Valla had taken my memories. But this was more intense. I felt like I'd briefly lost consciousness through the horrific pain, but luckily it didn't go on for long. I felt her hand being ripped from off my neck.

Coming more back around, I saw Relik was next to me, but his face was angry. "Why! Why did you come here, Gemma? I told you not too!"

"I'm so sorry Relik, I didn't mean to cause any harm. I was curious that's all," I cried.

"Well it is too late for sorry now, Gemma, she knows exactly where your body is. She has escaped back over to your realm and will be on route fast to get to it. She has now become a stealer, there is no reaching her. She is lost to us forever," he cried. He bowed his head. "We were doing healing on her and it was working until she sensed you."

"Oh, my god, Relik! I'm so sorry, what can I do, there must be something?"

"No, there is nothing, Gemma. I will need to become a swap for a person and try to get to Valla before Aluna does."

Alarmed I asked, "What will happen then?"

"I will have to try and trap her inside with me, in the body I take over in a swap," he replied turning away.

"Is that dangerous?"

He slowly turned to face me his expression sad it broke my heart. "Yes, extremely. I will then try and bring her back with me to the Detention pit. Unfortunately, I will be trapped there with her. Or possibly worse."

"No, no, Relik! I refuse to let you do this for me. I would rather stay here till my bloody body dies. Let her take my body, you're not going to sacrifice yourself for me. Especially when this is my fault in the first place." I could not believe he would consider such an act to protect me. There was a heartbreaking silence.

"It's okay, Gemma, I want to do this, I care a lot about you. I believe like I said before, you are special even if you don't believe it yourself." He put his hand on my face gently caressing it. "Anyway, she is my sister, if anyone should do this then it should be me."

"No, Relik, there has to be another way, what if I call Valla now and get quickly back into my own body?" I asked hopeful.

"Gemma, no! I'm sorry but that would only alert her to you sooner. She would take over your body in an instant, throwing out Valla, before you even got chance to return inside. This really is the only way I'm afraid." His tone of voice sounded full of authority.

"But can't she take over the body of whoever you become a swap for?"

"Yes, she can, Gemma, and if she does it's going to be a struggle keeping her from not overthrowing me. If I don't succeed, I will no longer exist any more. Stealers don't just throw you out from that body it normally destroys your whole essence too."

I looked stunned. In somewhat a daze I didn't know what to reply to that. Relik touched my arm, as he did an overwhelming feeling of love descended over me. In that very moment, I realized I had fallen for him. I could not let him do this, there had to be another way. He looked strangely at me and I realized he knew exactly how I felt about him. He hesitated as if he was going to say something but instead he shook his head and flew fast off. Upset, I gathered he'd left to see if there was a calling for a swap. I quickly searched for someone I could talk to about this. I floated swiftly along the beach, looking desperately for anyone. I luckily saw a few Kachinas a little further up from me.

When I reached them, they already knew what I was thinking. "There is one idea we could try, Gemma, but it's very risky and has a high chance of failure."

The nearest to me answered. "It has to be better than losing Relik like this. I'd risk anything right now! What can be done?"

There was a pause. "We could try and trick Aluna into doing a swap with someone who's dying."

"How would that work?"

"Sometimes, when a person in your realm is dying a long and painful death, they call out for a swap to take their place when the pain gets too much for them to bear. The soul will remain here till near the moment before their body dies. We don't feel pain in the same way as you do, Gemma, and we can switch a lot of it off in the human body. But it's emotionally draining and scaring for a Kachina. We don't want to go through it often. But a stealer will only want to have a swap with a healthy body so it can get as long as possibly in that body. If we can somehow find a dying person wanting a swap who's willing to help us, we could fool Aluna into thinking there's nothing wrong with them."

"Has it ever been done before?" I asked, hopeful the answer was what I wanted to hear.

"No never!" was his solemn reply.

The Kachinas in the meeting had already picked up on Relik's departure. To my relief, they told me not to worry, it wasn't too late, and the plan could work. A Kachina called Sion, the same one who had informed me Relik had gone was going to help. She would access the memories of someone still in Sanctuary who wanted to return to their body. But she would only take memories from before they had come here. Hopefully, Aluna wouldn't realize these memories were from someone who'd already been to Sanctuary.

Sion would hang onto the memories until a dying person could be found willing to do a swap. But they couldn't wait for one to come to them they needed help from a Seraph. Although this was unheard of and they risked trouble from the Enlightened circle.

Plus, it depended on whether the Seraph was even willing to help them; they would be powerless to do anything if they refused. A hell of a lot was riding on this. I was overwhelmed with anxiety as they consulted with a Seraph, the waiting for its answer was unbearable. After a tense time, the decision was yes and things were set into motion. The idea was to transport the memories collected from a girl which Sion found, into a dying female's mind. The memories not belonging to them would then be removed later from the soul. This of course providing it even worked, as it had never been tried before. There was uncertainly too whether the human mind could endure something on this kind of scale. But at this moment in time, it was their only option. I felt so nervous; I didn't want anyone else to suffer harm for something I'd done. If only Relik would have let me be trapped here for the rest of my life instead. After all, it was what I truly deserved!

Another Kachina was needed to do a swap immediately, so they would be able to track down where Relik was. I was told his name was Jaydin. With any luck Aluna would already be trapped inside with Relik. Jaydin would somehow need to get them to a fairy ring.

A girl that Sion had drawn memories from left to return to her own body. Now there was no trace of her ever being here. The waiting game then began!

It was agony waiting, but finally the Seraph found a dying woman and after revealing the choice for her pain to ease, she more than happily agreed to a swap. If only more people were aware of the existence of Kachinas I thought to myself. I prayed so hard it would work.

The Seraph took Sion to the woman, so she could plant false memories from the other girl into her mind. She apologized repeatedly to the woman for the extra pain she was now in. Luckily it seemed to have worked, at least so far.

A Kachina who had swapped bodies with Jaydin brought a note from him to us. One of the elders passed it to me. I read it aloud in my head, knowing the others could read my thoughts. It said:

Relik, in a host body managed to get in time to Valla who was still inside Gemma's body. Aluna homed in on her moments after. She came in through the ceiling in a glowing small blue mist. A dramatic fight then began. Gemma's gran managed to keep Aluna at bay from Valla with some crystals and chants she knew from the snails. It was just long enough for Relik to pull Aluna's essence inside his host with him. As I write this, they are fighting for dominance in that body. I fear we don't have long, I am not sure Relik can hang in there for much longer. Myself and Gemma's uncle have had to restrain Relik now for his own safety, as things have become quite violent. You must get Sion ready immediately after you receive this letter and onto the beach. I have gotten the woman who agreed to help waiting in the fairy ring which Gemma used to come to Sanctuary in.

I watched as Sion without a word, zipped off towards the beach. Now was time to see if this plan would really work or not. But the one thing I knew for sure, was the minute this was over, and I was certain Relik was safe. I would return immediately back to my own body. I was not going to risk something happening to Relik ever again. Not with everything he'd been willing to sacrifice for stupid old me.

If I still had legs I would have paced up and down the floor, but instead I zipped about here and there like a stunned fly. Finally, after what seemed like years, but in reality, was probably hours. I could see a Kachina in the distance coming towards us. I felt my heart in my throat as I tried to recognize who it was. I smiled when I realized it was Sion and rushed off to meet her. She smiled at me, but you could tell it was a smile tinted with sadness.

"Sion, what happened? Did it work?"

"Yes, Gemma, it did. We fooled her to take the body of the dying woman; she should only have a matter of weeks left in that body till she is returned here. This time she won't escape as the moment she crosses through the portal she will be transported into the detention pit." Sion bowed her head looking sad.

"Relik?" I dared asked. "How is he?"

"He's okay but is suffering the loss of his sister. Jaydin along with your uncle and gran got him into the fairy ring with Aluna still trapped within him. He was confused with what was happening and they couldn't let on anything or Aluna would know. Luckily, he trusts us, so he slightly let go his grip of Aluna within. In the moments before Sion pretended to take over the dying woman's body, Aluna feeling the chance to break free took the opportunity to get into the body first."

I stared at her. "What's happened to the dying woman's soul?"

"The Seraph has it and will take it wherever it should go at death."

I looked at Sion confused. "Why has Relik not returned with you?"

"He needs to stay there until you're ready to return or the body Aluna is in has died. Aluna didn't take the betrayal from us well at all. In fact, she was furious. She threatened Relik she would get revenge on everyone, including you. She believes Relik has chosen you over her. Relik tried to calm her down, but she escaped from them into the woods. They can't find her."

I closed my eyes so mad with myself. How could I expect Relik to ever forgive me?

"That's it, I am going back home. Then this will all be over and Relik can return. He does not deserve this."

"But, Gemma, you still have some healing to do, you're not ready yet."

"I am fine, Sion, but I won't be, if I have to live with the guilt of something else happening."

Chapter Ten

I held the crystal in the palm of my hand and called out to Valla that I wanted to return to my body. In a bright flash, suddenly my body stood there on the beach. I looked good with a new stylish haircut, a manicure and some new trendy looking clothes. Not bad I thought to myself, but probably not something I'd have normally gone for. But hey, it worked! "Are you really sure, you're ready to return back, Gemma? Relik is safe."

I nodded. "Yes, I am, I refuse to take any more chances. He's risked too much for me already."

"But, Gemma, you cannot return here until another five human years have passed. This is your best chance in recovering fully. I think you should reconsider it and maybe stay a little longer."

I was getting a touch concerned. Why was she saying this? Especially with everything she knew had recently happened. There was a small voice in the back of my head, nagging at me. Whose best interests was she thinking of, mine, Relik's, or maybe hers? This convinced me even more I should leave immediately. "No, Valla, I really do want to leave right now. I am so grateful to you and everyone here for everything. I will carry my time I have spent in here in my heart always. But I do feel I am recovered enough to return home."

Valla still reluctant replied, "Well, if you are certain, Gemma, we shall begin the swap back now."

I wasn't sure what should happen, other than we both agreed to return, and the crystal would again turn yellow. In another flash of light, I found myself back in my own body in the same fairy ring as before. I looked down at my hands, it all felt so strange to be in my own skin again. I looked around me, in the near distance I could see my Uncle Rob's car was just going to pull out of the woods. But it suddenly stopped, I watched as I saw my gran get out of the car. She called over. "Valla, over here, my dear where did you go? We were getting worried."

"Gran, no it's me, Gemma, not Valla," I shouted back.

Gran's face broke out with a beaming smile. She walked hastily over to me, flinging her arms tightly around me. "Oh, my sweet girl, I have missed you so much and we have been so worried about you. At one point, we even thought we might have lost you. I would have never forgiven myself, for encouraging you to do this in the first place. You cannot begin to imagine my relief, it has all worked out in the end. If it hadn't been for Relik and the others, you would have been trapped there." Gran hugged me tightly again.

The door on the passenger side of the car flung open. Stepping swiftly out was a man about nearly six-foot-tall in height. He was good looking, clean shaven with black short hair and warm large brown eyes. He walked fast over to me with a confused look etched on his face. "Gemma?" he said surprised in a deep Scottish accent.

I frowned. "Yes, but who are you?"

He smiled. "Well, my body's name is Russell. But it's me, Gemma, Relik!"

I didn't know whether to laugh or cry. I jumped up throwing my arms tightly around his neck I hugged him so tight not ever wanting to let go. Another guy then also got out from the car, shorter than Relik with light blue eyes and blonde hair parted in a curtains style. He quickly introduced himself to me as Jaydin. I hugged him tight too and thanked him sincerely for all his help.

The ride back to my gran's place, consisted of me and Relik looking almost starry eyed into each other's faces. There was a sexual tension burning between us both. But I suddenly remembered what Relik had lost because of me. "I'm so sorry, Relik, about your sister Aluna."

"Please don't be, as I am confident she was already lost to us on the beach of transition. Long before she had sensed you were there. She was too far gone. If I made you feel in any way to blame, then I am so sorry, it was because I was so upset at the time. Throughout the years that she was trapped over here, I had tried so hard to get any messages of love and hope over to her. I wanted her to still remember who and what she really was. For her to know I was doing whatever I could in Sanctuary to get her back home. It's such a risk for a Kachina to be trapped in a body for that long of a period. I'm sorry again, it really wasn't your fault, Gemma."

"You are too kind, Relik, I will be eternally grateful to you for everything you have done for me. I cannot imagine how I could ever pay you back."

He smiled through moist eyes as he took my hand holding it tight in his own. He leant over whispering with a huge smile. "I'd just settle for a kiss?"

I felt my cheeks glow hot as I blushed. Smiling, I whispered back, "I am more than happy to oblige, but maybe a bit more private."

He grinned nodding.

For the rest of the drive I thought on what this could mean. Could Relik have deep feelings for me too? Part of me didn't even dare hope this, as I wasn't sure my delicate heart could bear the strain if he didn't. But I was certain of one thing though and that was he did care about me.

Uncle Rob dropped Jaydin off first in the town center. Jaydin said he needed to return to Yorkshire where his host body lived. Relik and I got out the car. We went up and took turns giving him a hug.

"I will see you soon back in Sanctuary." Relik smiled.

"Yeah, Relik, soon. Bye, Gemma, take care."

I nodded. "I will try."

We waved to him as he walked off towards the train station. Secretly though, I hoped it wouldn't be too soon that Relik returned. I hoped we could spend some time together.

We arrived back at Gran's. It had felt like I'd been over in the other realm for months. But it was only three weeks back here. I felt so tired and hungry. Gran said she was going to make a nice pot of tea for everyone and some lunch. I went and sat at the table, Relik sat smiling next to me. I wished in some ways I could see the real beautiful him, but he still had such an alluring presence about him. I thought to myself even if he hadn't revealed to me who he was, I knew I would have soon realized it was him.

I wondered what had been going on while I had been away. What had Valla been doing as me? Had she done much, other than giving me the new look. "Much happened in the time I was away, what did Valla do being me? Did anyone guess anything different about me?" I said with a smile.

Gran stopped dead in her tracks and looked shocked at me. "Gemma, you should know all of that when you swapped back with Valla?"

Relik jumped up out of his chair. "Of course, Gemma, you should have already known who I was without needing to ask. I don't know why I didn't realize it was strange straight off." He paced up and down the floor and looked over at my gran with a confused look on his face.

Chapter Eleven

Relik looked at me his face still etched in worry. "Valla, for some reason didn't give you the memories of everything which had happened while she was you. She is meant to, it's a rule of the swap so you are aware of anything you should know about. To then be able to carry on fooling friends and family so they don't get suspicious you have not been yourself." Relik cursed out loud as he ran his fingers through his dark hair. Gran looked a little pale. "I can't think of any reason, why she would not have shown you her memories of her time with us. "Gemma, I wished I had told you what the normal practice was when you switched back. How the hell, did I forget to tell you such important stuff like that."

I felt concerned too remembering how hesitant Valla was to the swap back. At the time, I believed it was because she did not want to return yet. What the hell has she been up to while me? I moaned furiously to myself.

Gran told me Mum and Dad had not come down to visit me. They were going to, but she somehow managed to put them off. So, it wasn't as if I needed to fear anything there. Gran remembered Valla did have a brief phone call with my mum, but again nothing to worry about as she had pulled it off well. At least Gran had thought so at the time.

I noticed from the corner of my eye, my Uncle Rob was looking a little sheepish. "Uncle Rob, is there anything you might know?" I asked looking stern as I folded my arms.

He looked at me, rubbing his chin. "Well..." He paused. "Oh, dear god, Gemma. I really didn't think it would cause any harm. I am so sorry."

"What do you mean, Uncle Rob?" My throat suddenly felt dry and scratchy.

"She wanted to go out in the evenings. So, when your gran was asleep, I took her to a few places."

"Like where?" I shouted feeling this must be something to do with the reason she did not want me to know.

"Well, once to the cinema then another time bowling." He paused again, looking nervous. "One other time to a nightclub."

I couldn't reply immediately. But thinking this through it wasn't like anyone really knew me down in Devon. So, what if she'd had a few drinks and danced her socks off. Of course, with the way I had been lately before I had made the swap. It wouldn't have been something I'd have done, not with my depression and everything. I frowned. "Did you go with her to Uncle Rob? I wouldn't have thought it was your scene?"

"No, Gemma, but your cousin Cassy did."

Cassy was my uncle's daughter, which he'd had with an old girlfriend. She was twenty-three, just a year older than me. I'd see her maybe once or twice a year at family gatherings etc. We got on okay, and she seemed sensible most of the time. But she tended to be easily led if in the wrong crowd and she did not like to say no to anyone. Also like me she knew a lot of Gran's strange ways. Gran had been teaching her lately shaman healing and protection spells. I was sure she must have known and understood I had a Kachina inside me.

Gran glared madly at my worried Uncle Rob. "You stupid fool, what were you thinking?" she barked.

"I was sure Cassy would be able to keep a check on her, Mum. I am extremely sorry if something has happened to do with that." He sighed.

Relik suggested we should try and get hold of this Cassy and find out what in fact she knew. We tried calling her, but all we got was her annoying phone answer message. Uncle Rob, said he'd drive over to her place and see if he could find out anything. Gran followed him out to his car still moaning.

I went and sat nervously down at the table, one hand on my forehead. Relik poured me a hot cup of tea. I was certainly not hungry any more, it felt like my stomach had left my body, but with Relik comforting me, it felt a little reassuring, that things would be fine. I asked him what Valla's general character was like? He assured me she was a nice gentle and caring being. That this was not something he would have expected, especially coming from her. He said also that she had been a swap many times before, without any problems ever arising. I felt strangely so calmed, with just how he now had his arm gently around me in such a protective sort of way. I heard the sweet sincerity in his voice, just like how I had experienced back in the other realm. I felt a weird tingling sensation run down the back of my spine, along with my stomach feeling like it was full of butterflies as the old saying goes.

Suddenly from nowhere I felt faint. So I told him and Gran I needed to go and have a quick lay down. They both agreed it would be a good idea, so off I went up to my room. The moment my head hit the soft pillow I was out for the count.

While I was napping, Gran got chatting away with Relik. "You know, Relik, it could never workout for you."

He looked a bit puzzled by this comment, but quickly realised what she meant. "Yes, I am trying very hard to fight it but it is so difficult. This is not something on this magnitude, I have ever felt before. But I don't want to ever hurt her and yes I do realize it would be impossible." He bowed his head his face showed his anguish. "So you do agree, Relik, that when we find out what Valla is hiding from her, that you leave as soon as possible?" Relik reluctantly nodded.

"Though it is certainly a shame. as you would have been so good for her. But it's just the way things are, there is nothing any of us can do about it." Gran placed her hand on his shoulder rubbing it gently. He looked up at her with despair clear in his moist brown eyes.

Chapter Twelve

There was a little tap on the bedroom door where I was still resting. I said wearily to whoever it was that they could come in. The door handle slowly turned, and a red short haired woman casually walked inside.

"Cassy!" I said a little surprised to see her here already.

"Hiya, Gemma," she replied, but her tone did not seem happy. She sat down on the edge of the bed picking nervously at her brown woolen jumper sleeve. This straight off made me feel uneasy. "I am so sorry, Gemma, I did not realize she would go so far. I just thought she was having a bit of harmless fun. She had assured me, that she was not going to do anything too inappropriate to how you would have normally acted."

Cassy avoided any eye contact with me. Feeling my face grow hot I gripped the unicorn patchwork quilt with my hand tight in a fist, sitting bolt right up in the bed. "Okay what the bloody hell did she do, Cassy? Just tell me please right now!"

Cassy backed off and stood up. "Well… We went to a little nightclub, just on the outskirts of the town. To begin with we were just dancing having a drink or two, a laugh etc. When this cute guy, suddenly started chatting her up, she ended up leaving the nightclub with him. I did honestly try, Gemma, to stop her, but she was already gone off in his car before I could get over to her." She gulped hard. The colour in my face must have drained bad, as Cassy became extremely concerned. "Gemma, Gemma are you okay?" she cried placing her hand on my arm.

It took me a few more minutes to be able to get the words out, I blubbered for a bit. "Let me get this straight, what you're actually telling me is, Cassy... that Valla went off and had a flipping one-night stand with god knows who, in my bloody body! Is that right?" I asked as tears welled up in my hurt eyes.

"Yes, Gemma, I am so sorry, but I do believe so," she mumbled.

"Oh, my God!" I said as the room suddenly started spinning fast, and everything went black.

Things initially were somewhat a blur, but the first face I saw as I started to come back round, was poor Relik's concerned one. He was leaning over me sitting there on the bed. "Gemma, I truly don't know what to even say. I'm terribly sorry. Cassy has told us everything just after you passed out," Relik softly said his face full of sadness.

I tried sitting up but holding onto my head as I still felt a little dizzy. "Get Cassy back here right now! I need to talk to her," I screamed. But my gran who was now also already in the room, informed me, that Uncle Rob had already taken her back to her place. Gran said that she had thought that it was for the best. But that she had already shared some severe words with the pair of them.

"Oh no! But I didn't ask her?" I paused, as the very thought was suddenly way too scary to even think of.

"Gemma, you didn't ask what?" Relik asked anxiously.

Now I didn't even want to say, however, I slowly started to get the words out. "Did she?" I choked. "Did she... Oh god, did she at least use some bloody protection?" I squeaked.

Both my gran and Relik turned and looked back at each other. Did they already know? It was too hard for me to be able to tell from just the looks on their pasty faces? "No, Gemma, I'm afraid she didn't use any. Cassy did ask Valla that when she saw her the day after," Gran answered.

From the fuming look which was on my poor gran's face, my Uncle Rob might not be around for a while if he knew what was good for him. I sighed loudly and laid back down staring blankly up at the pretty ceiling. Relik in this moment in time, really wished he could read my mind in this realm seeing me lay there looking so lost and distressed. I felt his hand take mine and him hold it affectionately. After thinking long and hard about it, I guessed there really was only one thing for it.

Gran had managed to get an appointment at the doctors for tomorrow morning. But I had already checked my diary and believed that unless my period had been early, before I'd returned to my body, I was by now four days or so late. Normally this probably was not much of a worry for some people, but I was usually totally spot on with my dates. Then there were the other worrying thoughts that scared the hell out of me, what if I'd caught something nasty. How could Valla have seriously done this to me. I felt so violated and betrayed.

That evening Relik sat with me in Gran's little glass conservatory. It overlooked her magical garden. The snow had all gone but the early spring chill was in the air and I started feeling a little cold so I got up and closed an open window. Spreading slowly like a blanket over the garden lawn though, was a thick grey mist. This along with the full moon shining down on it, made it all seem even more mystical than usual. We sat there silent, I did not know what to even think or feel. Gran brought us all in some mugs of steaming hot chocolate, full of small colourful marshmallows. She glanced out into the garden as she placed the hot drinks down for us on the small, round, pine coffee table. "Oh, it certainly does look like it is going to be an extra special night tonight," she commented looking almost excited.

I frowned back up at her. "A night for possibly asking some questions do you think, Gran?"

"Could well be, Gemma, I think the nature sprite snails will definitely be about tonight with the added energy of the full moon and that mist. Myself and Relik should go out and see if they are willing to enlighten us at all?" Gran gave me a little wink.

"Umm I want to come with you too." Sounding like I was coming with them regardless.

"Oh, no, sweetheart, you're certainly not. What you need to do is sit and relax with the hot chocolate. You have had a nasty shock, my dear. While you take it easy, we will try and see if they are in a good talking mood tonight. As you know they don't like to be bothered. Plus, they have yet to still speak to you," Gran replied.

I sat there feeling pretty pissed off and sure my face showed it. I knew deep down as usual she was right. One day they may deem me as being worthy of their wisdom. But until then I'd just have to settle on my gran and Relik gaining their insight on the unknown and unnatural things. Relik lent down and kissed my cheek ever so gently as he went to leave out the door with my gran. I smiled at up at him reaching quickly out for his hand. I held on to it for a moment. He smiled before gently pulling away. I watched him follow Gran.

In the garden my gran led Relik through the mist to the stone rockery, where she'd on occasions encountered the snails. Something small suddenly ran right through Relik's legs tugging at his trousers. He looked but saw nothing. "It was probably a gnome Relik they love to prank people, mischievous little devils." Gran laughed. But suddenly she went quiet, pointing to something on top of the rockery. It was a large silver shelled snail. Anyone else would have thought it was a plain garden variety snail. But it was a beautiful silver colour, its shell engraved with such detail. Like Jack the griffin had said it glowed slightly in the now dark evening. But this was certainly not the only difference it had to a normal snail. Provided it was in the right mood and willing to give you some of its knowledge, its tiny mouth would open and close as it would talk to you. That was if you were someone they saw as deserving this honour.

"Nature sprite, I do wonder if you would please give us some advice, from the supernatural world?" Gran asked it.

Nothing happened apart from that the snail kept rising up and down from its shell, as if it was trying to take a better look at Relik. After a few minutes had passed, it did then speak. "Kachina, you are very far from home. Why is this still? Are you leaning towards becoming a stealer?"

"No of course not, I am only still here trying to help Gemma, I was her guide back in my realm and I still feel a duty with all that has happened. Especially now with Valla, I want to try and fix things. I do intend to return back soon to Scotland, from where this body that I'm in normally lives!"

"What! You stupidly think Kachina for one moment you can fool me? You have completed your mission here to stop your sister. The rest has absolutely nothing to do with you. You should have already left this body and returned back to Sanctuary." There was a pause. "You are trying to cover the real reason for you remaining here. But you risk too much unnecessary pain, for her and yourself. Though you already know this. So, leave right now! Your union cannot be, unless you are intending to take the wrong path?"

Relik looked upset by these harsh comments, he bowed his head. "I will never take that path, I can assure you of that. I know I must leave I just wanted a little more time with her. If you are trying to say I must leave before I fall love with her, then it's already too late."

Crash! I nearly tripped right over the garden wheelbarrow from where I was secretly hiding and listening to their conversation. Both Gran and Relik looked behind them confused from where the noise had come from.

"Tell your granddaughter, to come closer," the snail unexpectedly growled.

Gran looked angrily over her shoulder. "Gemma, what did I tell you? Come here right now, child!"

The snail started chuckling which got louder, it was a strange jolly sort of laugh, not like something you would have suspected to come out from something so small. After it had composed itself it said, "What did you expect old woman, that the misguided girl would just sit there sipping away the hot drink?"

Poor Relik would not even look at me as I got closer to them. My heart was beating so incredibly fast with excitement, I already was in love with him. I had allowed myself to think he felt something on them lines for me. But having it confirmed made me feel like break dancing on the moon with happiness.

"As you have already heard, girl, this is not a possible relationship. In fact, it's doomed to be nothing more than a serious heartbreak. It will unquestionably destroy the both of you. If you do not come to terms with this we may have to intervene."

"Thanks for not sugar coating it," I barked.

Relik turned and looked sadly at me his eyes moist with tears. "He is right, Gemma, to save any more suffering to the both of us. I should leave now." A single tear dripped down his cheek.

I stared deep into his brown eyes. "But I love you too and I still need you here." Tears started overflowing in my own eyes.

Relik looked as if he was going to fall to pieces and took me in his arms. He held me so tight I could feel his heart beating as if it was going to explode. "I'm so sorry."

Before I knew it, he ran out through the garden gate. I went to run after him but was grabbed by Uncle Rob. I struggled hard to try and break free. "Let him go, Gemma, it's the right and only thing to do in this situation!"

"No!" I screamed still trying to get away. "This is not fair there has to be something we can do to be together," I cried as I looked down at the bloody snail.

"I'm afraid not, Gemma. Soon the soul back in his realm will want to return to its real body. Then Relik must return the body back to him. He has already broken all the rules by not staying in Scotland and pretending to live like Russell would have. Also, I'm guessing he more than likely did not tell you, he cannot be a swap for another person for five human years, just like you cannot go back to Sanctuary for five years either. So even if you did steal a little time with each other, it would only be for maybe a few days here and there. Then, a five-year break between each time."

"But I could live with that, at least it would be something. Anything would be better than nothing," I cried.

"Think seriously about what you are saying, Gemma. When someone does a swap, they want you to become them for a while. Live their lives till they are ready to return back to them. Not to mistreat their body to some great love affair. Which unfortunately you know yourself to be unfair and which now brings me to answer your next question. Yes, you are pregnant!"

Chapter Thirteen

If the ground could have swallowed me up whole, now would have been a good time. Uncle Rob managed to somehow catch me in the nick of time as I fainted. I then spent the next week or so sitting in my room in complete silence, reverting slowly back to my previous depression. Gran had bought four pregnancy tests, not that she really doubted the snail was right, but just so we could see it for ourselves. Each one of them of course being positive. I still needed to see the doctor, I had not had anything else ruled out either with possible diseases. But my gran was unsure of how to get me there in this state. Just to make matters worse, my parents were coming down to see me.

A few days later Mum and Dad turned up just in time for Gran's famous bacon and special sauce sandwiches. But just the smell made me want to hurl, morning sickness was kicking in. I was having a lie down when my door knocked. "Come in."

"Hi, sweetheart, how are you doing?"

I sat up in the bed trying to beat the nausea. "Hi, Mum, yeah I am doing better."

She put her arms around me. "That's great, honey, your dad and I could not be happier."

Mum said thought she'd heard the old me in the last phone call we had shared. If only she really knew, I thought painfully to myself as I wondered if it was before, or after Valla had screwed some complete bloody stranger. Mum said she'd let me get some sleep, but that my dad was really looking forward to seeing me. I guessed that I'd better put in an appearance, as not to raise any suspicions. I did not want to go back home just yet as I was clinging on to a silly thought, that just maybe he would come back to me.

While I had yet another very unpleasant visit to the toilet bowl, Dad asked my gran, if she was laying off telling me all about the usual spiritual, fairy tale kind of stuff that she would normally feed me. Gran assured him that there was no funny business going on. If only my poor dad knew the truth. He'd completely flip out I thought as I had overheard the conversation, while walking down the long hall to the kitchen. "Gemma!" my dad said out loud as he'd quickly got up and out of the chair, flinging his arms around me as I'd walked in.

"Hey Dad," I replied in a fake tone.

"We're all really missing you back home, sweetheart. Donna sends you her love, but of course as usual we couldn't drag her away from her latest boyfriend. I do so worry about that crazy girl sometimes." His tone changed to one of genuine concern.

I suddenly had a nasty flashback of the potential tunnels and that terrible image, the one of Donna taking drugs. I knew for sure that I could not allow that to ever happen. Not to my baby sister.

I sat down at the table in the middle of Dad and Gran, trying to put on a brave face. Mum smiled. "We brought your gifts today as your dad can't make it up for your birthday, he already had made plans for a golfing weekend. Mum gave Dad then one of her looks and he sank down into his chair. He then glanced up at me. "It was a mistake, I should have remembered to keep that date free, so I apologise darling."

"It's okay dad, no worries I am going to be twenty-two not like twenty-one or something." I went dead quiet, that was not a birthday I ever wanted to remember. Everyone was silent for a few moments.

Mum reached into her bag and pulled out two boxes wrapped in gift paper. "Okay, sweetie, here you go we hope you like them." She passed them to me while she hunted about still in her bag as if looking for something.

I opened one and then the box inside. In that box was a necklace, it was real gold with a beautiful unicorn pendant. I smiled, thinking how fitting it was after being among real ones.

"I love it, guys, thanks so much."

Mum got out of her chair, here let me put in on for you. I nodded. Lifting my hair, she placed it around my neck and hugged me. Sitting back down she looked again in her handbag. "I am sorry, sweetheart, I have left your card back at home. When we get back I will post it to you."

"Okay, Mum, that's fine."

"Open your other one then. Your sister helped pick it out for you," Dad said.

I opened that and the box too and pulled out a small crystal covered dreamcatcher with small white feathers.

Dad leaned over and hugged me. "She thought maybe it could help with your bad dreams."

"Oh, that's so thoughtful and kind. Thanks again."

Gran got up from the table. As we are doing gifts today I am going to get mine for you." She smiled before disappearing back into the house.

After a few moments she returned with a large box. She passed it to me. I wondered what it was. Opening the box and put my hands inside and pulled out a large, heavy, crystal ball. Gran then reached inside the box and picked out a stand to place it on. I looked at it strangely for a moment unsure what to say.

"Mum, what have I said about this kind of thing. She is training to be a doctor not some gypsy fortune teller." Dad said, his voice sounding a little harsh.

"Oh, Steven, don't start! This has been passed down by generations of my father's family. And she can use alternative methods alongside traditional medicine."

"Right, stop it, guys! And Gran, I love it and will take good care of it."

Gran smirked almost at dad as she sat back down and as normal he rolled his eyes.

Mum and Dad stayed a little longer, we all went and sat together in the garden for a while. Dad was strangely looking at a couple of snails; he was kind of looking at them suspiciously as they sat there on the small stone wall that surrounded the patio area. I wondered to myself why the interest. Had he ever met a talking snail. I never liked snails much before, but now I couldn't stand the little bastards.

It had started getting colder and I was also getting worried they would never leave. Finally, Dad said, "I think we should be heading back, we have a long drive ahead and the traffic here was something terrible." Mum agreed and went to find her handbag, which she was forever leaving somewhere and forgetting. When they were all set, I kissed my parents goodbye. But secretly I wished I could take my mum somewhere quiet and tell her everything. Especially with the added dilemma I was also in with the baby. But just for now, I knew I needed to pull myself enough together to go and see the doctor.

Chapter Fourteen

Gran took me there next morning, she had wanted to come in with me, but I had insisted I wanted to go in alone. The doctor sat there and listened as I told him, how I'd shamefully got drunk and had a one-night stand, that not only was I pregnant but also very worried about other things. I was sure from his smug expression he'd seen it all before. I got the impression that he was thinking yet another silly young woman who's gone and got herself up the duff. But man, was he seriously mistaken. I was in a truly messed up situation.

Five minutes later, I'd already seen a nurse and had a swab and all the necessary blood taken. I wondered as I rubbed my sore arm, if I had any blood left. Now I'd just have to wait an anxious week or so, for the results to come back. In the meantime, he'd arranged for me to see a midwife. Jesus this so wasn't happening to me, I thought sadly on the way back in the car.

Back inside the house I sat down, my thoughts yet again were back to Relik. I so wished that he was still here with me. I really needed him even more so now than I could ever imagine. Gran asked me what I wanted to do, did I want to go ahead with the pregnancy and keep the baby. I said the doctor had asked me the same thing. I had told him yes, that it wasn't the poor innocent child's fault.

But I was in serious turmoil over it all deep inside. This was not something I could have conceived of happening to someone like me. Especially, when I was back in the other realm. It really was so dangerous having a swap with a Kachina, you could possibly return to a readymade family or all kinds of other unforeseen predicaments. Carrying on with medical school was now not going to happen, everything was gonna have to be put on hold. Mum and Dad were going to be so disappointed with me when they found out. The worse thing though was, not ever being able to tell the poor kid who its father could be in the future.

One night when me and Gran had gone to bed, I was suddenly awoken by a strange noise coming from downstairs. Wearily I listened to what sounded like a party. It sounded like people laughing and talking loudly. I could not believe my gran was having a late-night party, especially as I'd thought that she was already in bed. But even more so, she had not even told me about it. I listened for a few more moments, before trying to get out of the bed to go and fully investigate. But I felt so tired almost unnaturally drowsy, like however much I wanted to get up it was impossible. The exhaustion overcome me. and I drifted off into a deep sleep. I vividly remember the dream I had to this very day.

I was downstairs right in the middle of some party. I realized I was small again maybe about five, I was wearing my favourite pink bunny pajamas. There were a lot of people I did not recognize crammed inside my gran's house. Some were drinking what looked like wine, a few smoking cigars and others just talking and laughing. I then saw sitting at the dining room table, two men playing chess. One of the men stopped and looked up at me smiling. He was stocky built like he knew what a hard day's work was. Hard to say how tall as he was sitting, but he didn't look short. Brown, messy curly hair that needed a haircut covered his blue shirt collar. "Ah, there you are, my little Gemma, do you want to learn how to play chess?" he asked with a cocky half smile. I nodded, thinking as I looked at him he seemed strangely familiar. There was something uncanny with his brown eyes really reminded me of someone. The other man nodded and quickly got up and left the table. The guy gestured to me to sit down, so I went and sat in the other man's place. He then showed me how to play. I caught on quick and he seemed very impressed. "You're just like Robbie, he caught on quick and even beat me a few times." He grinned looking even more familiar.

After another few rounds, I yawned.

"You better be going to bed, sweetheart, your grandma going to be cross with me I keep you up so late."

I nodded and yawned again before I felt strong arms pick me up and carry me up to the little attic room. He gently lowered me down in the bed before pulling my duvet over me. He kissed my forehead. "Goodnight sweetheart, I have left you something under your bed as a reminder of tonight. You're a special little lass just wish you believed it. Now don't forget me, will you?"

I smiled at him. Half sleepy I replied, "I won't."

I woke up from the dream feeling like it was too unbelievably real.

Jumping out of bed I grabbed my robe. I was just about to leave the room when I remembered, rushing over I looked beneath the bed. I gasped as I reached for it. In my hand, I now held a black queen, chess piece. I was stunned. I ran downstairs and went into the living room. On Gran's mantel piece, she had family photos. I scanned them for his face. Then I saw him he was holding my dad as a little boy. I ran into the kitchen, she was there singing to herself as she cooked bacon and eggs. "Umm, Gran, in this photo this is Grandad, isn't it?"

Gran turned and took hold of the photo. "Yeah, the love of my life, no one better." She smiled but with tears in her eyes, before serving up us both a plate of food. Luckily my nausea was not as bad today.

"Gran just before I fell asleep, I swear I heard a party down here, but something stopped me getting out of bed. I then fell in a deep sleep, but I had the most vivid dream. I was small again and he was in it. I felt safe and loved and he taught me how to play chess. Putting me to bed, he said he would leave me something under my bed, so I don't forget. I woke up and remembered so many details, even how he smelled like cigars, and the twinkle in his eyes. I then found this chess piece under my bed."

I opened my hand and showed it to her. My gran now had tears rolling down her pink cheeks.

"Yeah he loved his cigars once a week. He would often to have friends over for a drink and a game of his favourite chess."

I put my arm around her. "He said he taught Uncle Robbie too."

She nodded. "Yeah your dad didn't seem too interested in chess he preferred his time with his dad fishing."

Gran looked at the chess piece. "Hold on a sec?"

I let go of her as she went out the kitchen and into the living room. She picked up her phone and rang someone. "Rob, go check your chess set that was your dad's. See if the queen is missing." There was a pause.

"Okay, well it's here, Gemma has it. Come over with the set, it would seem she had a special visitor last night. See I told you she is a gifted one. Okay, bye." She hung up the phone and smiled at me.

When Uncle Rob turned up I told him everything I had told my Gran. I then handed him his chess piece. He looked it over carefully. "Amazing, Gemma, I am so pleased he visited you. You must take notice as even the other side are trying to help you." He grinned. "Come on then, let's have a few games of chess and Mum if you have any spare egg and bacon I wouldn't say no."

"Coming right up." Gran beamed.

Shockingly I beat him twice. He was stunned. "Remind me not to bet with cash with Gemma in the future." He laughed.

Chapter Fifteen

After Uncle Rob had stuffed his face with more fried eggs and bacon than I could ever eat in a week, he got up from the chair and said, "See you later, earthlings."

I got dressed in some jeans and pink sweater and went into the garden. It was early spring, but flowers were blooming already which would only normally be in warmer months. It was amazing how much things came to life in Gran's own little Sanctuary. The garden was big and towards the back was an apple and plum orchard. Best tasting fruit, I have ever eaten. She also had a vegetable patch which was always filled with all kinds of varieties of veg. Gran certainly had green fingers, but she would always say it was the gnomes that did everything in the garden. That she did not have to lift a finger, in thanks for letting them live in her garden. I laughed at the thought of little garden gnomes running around with their little wheelbarrows of seeds and planting all matter of things. I got up and decided to take a walk down to the orchard as behind it was a large overgrown pond. It had a mini waterfall that Uncle Rob had made himself out of colourful rocks. The water was crystal clear and some beautiful lily pads floated on the top. Koi carp goldfish swarm up to the top thinking I had food for them.

I sat down on the long grass and listened to the pouring water sound, trying to let it take my cares away. I smiled as an old memory of my childhood came into my mind. I was about seven and playing hide and seek round the trees with Donna, when I saw a glittering shape hovering above her head. Then another and another one appeared. I told Donna don't move. I slowly got closer but I was shocked to see what appeared to be tiny, blue winged, creatures with what seemed to be silver fish tails. I told Donna to look up as they darted in the air all around us. Getting even closer I could make out the top half of them had an almost cute humanoid appearance. I even swore one smiled at me before they all flew off towards the pond. We ran back inside to Gran and told her. I remember her laughing saying they were Merfairies that live in her pond. Gran seemed so excited. I remembered her saying you're blessed if they show themselves to you. She also said, whatever you do don't tell your father. Over the years, I just figured we must have seen some kind of colourful dragonflies. Now of course I knew what we saw must have been real. I mean come on talking bastard snails, how couldn't they be real. I hoped if I sat here long enough one may appear but after a while I got tired and getting back up I walked back to the house.

Gran made a pot of tea and I sat at the kitchen table. "Penny for your thoughts?"

"I was just thinking why Dad has never seen or believed what lives here."

"Some people can't handle stuff like this, so they switch off to it. Others are gifted and more open minded.

I tried hard in the beginning when he was small to show him things, but when I saw the fear in his eyes I knew I had to stop. Same fear I once saw with your sister Donna, when she saw a gnome. You can't force these things on people. With your Uncle Rob, it was completely different. From the age of two he would be outside talking to the snails, so I knew he had the gift." She paused. "As do you."

I smiled. "Not so sure now if I would call it a gift or a curse."

She rubbed my shoulders. "It's going to be okay, sweetie and you'll get through this. There is so much more I want to teach you."

She passed me a mug of tea. I sat there for a moment then looked at my hand. It was gone and I never took it off. It was Valla's fault. I started to cry.

Gran held me. "Whatever is the matter, child, tell me?"

"My ring that Neil gave me, I always wore it I never took it off. It was a promise ring, that we'd always be together," I said between sobs.

"Okay, well you go and look if she put in anywhere in your room, but if not, don't worry as I have a plan."

I dabbed my eyes and went upstairs to look. There was no sign of it. I went back down my face told my gran she needed to use her plan then.

***

In a corner of the garden, there was hidden a deep limestone wishing well. It was covered by some thick prickly bramble brushes. Gran informed me that it contained a friendly, but powerful water Jinn. That if you ever lost something special to you, then this was the place to come. Because if you threw into the water something sweet which it really loved, the water Jinn in return would go and find your lost item for you. Normally the next day you would find it on or near to your bed.

So, I decided to give it a try. I went and threw into the well a couple of Gran's favourite hard boiled fruit sweets. I listened patiently to hear them drop down into the water, but strangely heard nothing. I really hoped it worked as I went off to bed that night. The next morning low and behold, it was there on my bedside cabinet. I held it in my hand trying to take it in. I had heard nothing come into my room that night. I put it back on my finger but felt bad for my feelings for Relik. But he was right when he said that Neil would not want me to grieve for him forever. Plus, you can't help it if you fall in love.

Downstairs Gran was making breakfast, this time just some porridge. Gran looked down at my hand. "Great, you got it back, I was sure you would. Got to love that Jinn."

I stared out the kitchen window towards where the well was. "What does it look like?"

"I can't say, but some say it is a shape shifter that in this realm it never took a permeant form."

I felt confused. "Not sure I understand though, but okay."

Gran put her arm around and pulled me close to her "There is a lot that none of us will ever understand, Gemma."

Relik unknown to me at the time, was still here in my realm and still inside Russell's body. He'd wanted desperately to come and see me, but he felt it was for the best he didn't. But every day he had stayed waiting for Russell to call him back, he cursed it, as it was another day wasted that we could be together.

One day, as Relik, was in his hide out he heard what sounded like his name called. He turned around in the distance he could see a petite blonde woman running very fast towards him.

"Relik!" she shouted.

As she got closer he sensed it was Sion, an ability he still had in this body to be able too.

"Relik we have a big problem!" She paused catching her breath. "It's your sister Aluna, she escaped as she was being transported to the dark place. The body she was in died sooner than was expected. We also back in Sanctuary, believe she has gained extra knowledge of how to resist the pull of the dark place."

Relik looked shocked. "Has she already taken over another Kachina?"

Sion wiped a tear away face. "Yes, Relik, I'm afraid we have lost Jaydin and another one I did not know. After she had thrown Jaydin out his host body, she disposed of the body by throwing herself in front of a train. She then took over Emilia's swap body and now possesses that somewhere."

Sion started to weep. Relik took her in his arms and hugged her tight. "I am so sorry for your loss, Sion. Your brother was such a good friend to me; he will be missed by all who were lucky enough to know him."

He suddenly stopped dead in his tracks. Aluna's threat, he anxiously thought to himself, why hadn't he taken it seriously enough. "Gemma!" he shouted. "I must see that she is okay." He began running fast as he could to my gran's place. Sion was not far behind him. He banged hard on the front door, but there was no answer. Me and my gran had popped into the town for some shopping. She somehow had managed to convince me to come out with her, lying I felt that her back was really aching her. Relik was getting frantic with worry. But he knew it was only a small town, prayed he would be able to find me and quickly. Gran and I had just left her local butcher's, she had wanted to get some lamb for the Sunday roast. She made the best roast lunches ever and even though I had morning sickness, I was still looking forward to it. We were chatting away as we walked slowly down the small narrow cobbled street. "Gemma! Is that you?" a man's voice with a foreign accent asked just behind me and Gran.

I turned quickly round to see who it was. A man in his late twenties, tall with dark features and olive skin was walking up to us. "Yes, I'm Gemma," I said as I tried to recognize him. Oh, my god, I suddenly thought what if he was the father of my baby. Unfortunately, I discovered this was not the case as I felt the blade go in.

A large kitchen knife had stabbed me, I felt an agonizing pain pierce deep into my stomach. Suddenly it felt as if everything was going in slow motion as I hit the pavement. Then I heard his lovely voice. I tried desperately not to pass out. "Gemma!" Relik shouted again as he crouched down by my side. I lay motionless on the ground, feeling very lightheaded a load of blood pooling next to me on the path. Sion was running as fast as she could to get over to me. But before she got any closer she was sent flying hard across the road. The man who had just stabbed me was still here and he had rammed himself directly into Sion. Relik got quickly to his feet and faced him. His face was full of thunder as Relik went straight for him. The man was still holding the knife as they fought. Relik had got some good punches in but the man drove the blade hard straight into his neck, as he tried in vain to get the weapon off him. The body that Relik was in slumped to the ground not far from me. My poor gran screaming had already run back into the butcher's to alert the emergency services.

Russell's body Relik, had just been in was now sadly dying. Relik himself had been instantaneously transported back to Sanctuary in the nick of time before Russell died. He materialized on the beach of transition very traumatized. Frantically he begged and pleaded with the elder Kachinas to let him return immediately. "But you know you cannot for another five years, you know the rules, Relik. You cannot keep being a swap, you need to rest and not get too used to having such a more corporeal body. As you already know yourself, we found that it would increase a Kachina's chances of becoming a stealer."

"But you don't understand, I need to get back to Gemma she is dying. Aluna is on the rampage, she is after revenge on us all. Sion will be next and a lot of people and Kachinas are going to die! Do you understand what I am saying? She will keep on killing human bodies and taking over and destroying us. She has become the most powerful stealer we may have ever known. She must be stopped, or this may never end!"

They thought hard about it. After some consideration, it was decided to let Relik return in the next swap available. But there was a condition, that instead of killing the host body she was now in, because of Aluna's terrible crimes against other Kachinas and humans, he needed to throw out her essence, eradicating her forever.

He would need to learn the skills to do this, but even they were unaware of how to do this. Relik had an idea who may be able to help him with this. He told them that beings in my realm would know. But first he needed to return to me. He suddenly panicked what if he was too late, what if I was dead. He could not bear to think it.

Chapter Sixteen

In the hospital, it was touch and go for me as I clung onto life. I'd lost a hell of a lot of blood and had some slight damage to my liver. I had also lost the baby. Gran never left my side and Mum, Dad and Donna soon turned up. Mum with tears running down her cheeks, held my hand as I started to slowly come back round.

"Relik, where's Relik?" I whispered confused trying to cling onto my consciousness.

Mum stared at Gran. "Who is she talking about?"

Gran seemed to hesitate to reply to her. "Oh… just a friend she has met, umm, he lives down the road from me, very nice chap."

The police were here and trying to piece things together. Gran and Sion had come up with a good explanation of events between them both. They told the police they believed it was a mugging, that had gone terribly wrong. That the guy had gone for my purse, but I'd fought him back and he'd stabbed me. That Russell was just a bystander they pretended not to know, who had bravely tried to intervene. But that he had been stabbed too in the process. The police told them regrettably they now needed to inform Russell's family back in Scotland of his death.

They both gave a good description of the stabber, even though Sion thought to herself it would make no difference in catching him. More than likely Aluna would have already discarded that body and thrown out yet another Kachina getting herself a new body. Sion needed to try and track her down even though the police had asked her to make herself available for some further questions.

Relik, in the meantime, swapped with a guy named Scott. He lived in London, so it was going to take Relik five to six hours to get back down to Devon by car, so the train seemed his best bet. After grabbing a bag, he quickly filled it with some of Scott's clothes and things he may need, before heading off fast to the station.

Scott was an interesting character. In his late twenties, he was what you may describe as a biker, heavy metal dude. He was a big guy, six foot four and very muscular. He had long dark hair tied back in a ponytail, a goatee beard and light tanned skin. On one of his arms he had a detailed viper snake tattoo. He looked somewhat menacing apart from the indisputable warmth that shone in his dark brown eyes and a grin that engulfed his dimpled face. Wearing all black leather gear and a silver earing he was a bit too stereotypical for Relik's liking. The train ride down to Devon was interesting to say the least. People he was sharing the carriage with were unnerved by his presence. Most had quickly moved to the front of the carriage even though there was more room back where he was. This was something Relik was not accustomed to. But he tried to not let it bother him and most of the trip he was just miles away in deep thought, thinking only about me. He considered that if I was already dead, what would be the point any more. But part of him still knew taking Aluna over, would be saving others he also cared for. He just wished that he would still have the strength needed to succeed, if I was truly gone.

The train finally pulled into the station, Relik waiting was getting impatient for the automatic doors to open. He smacked the door hard with the palm of his hand, shouting, "Come on, open up." When they finally parted he leapt off and bounded fast up the concrete steps to the main street. He had checked a map beforehand, the only hospital in Gran's town was luckily just a few blocks away from the station. He ran like lightning, nearly sending some old geezer flying as he quickly dodged him. His heart was beating so fast, and the sweat was running down his face as he neared the hospital entrance. Mum and my dad had gone for a quick coffee, while Gran and Donna sat with me. At the reception desk, Relik out of breath asked where I was. A nurse told him but said only relatives could visit at present.

Relik replied, "It's okay I am her brother," as he legged it to the lift. I was on the third floor, bay seven as a big guy suddenly pulled back the curtain surrounding my bed. Gran near enough jumped right out of her chair and Donna looked completely terrified.

"How is she? Please tell me she going to be okay?" he asked, his face full of concern.

Gran paused, looking inquisitively deep into his brown eyes.

"The answer you seek, is yes, it is me, Relik,"He said before she could get the words out. Donna, was still rooted hard to her chair looking confused as hell.

"Donna, my dear, could you go and see where your mum and dad have got to and if you could get us all some water please?" Gran asked looking pleadingly at her. Donna very slowly got up and started to walk off, still not able to take her eyes off Relik, the whole time as she turned the corner. After she had finally gone, Relik came closer to me. I was still asleep, but I suddenly woke as if I somehow strangely knew he was there.

"How are you feeling?" he softly said. I looked up at him and smiled, recognizing straight off that Relik was inside this body. My connection with him was strong, I was certain I would always know him anywhere.

"I am much better now I have my knight in heavy metal with me," I said not able to resist the cheesy comment and smiling with the little strength I had remaining.

He smiled before lightly kissing my forehead with his warm lips, just as my mum and dad walked back in. Dad's face was a picture. He looked stunned at Donna, then back over to me, as if he was thinking and all this time I've been worrying about the guys Donna hangs out with. My mum's eyebrow raised high as she came closer to me. To be honest it was kind of funny really, I just wished I wasn't in so much pain.

Everyone was quiet and they all seemed nervous. "Well, if no one is going to speak I will introduce Relik to you myself," I croaked in a small voice breaking the tension in the air.

"Guys, this is my very good friend Relik. Relik, this is my parents and my sister, Donna."

I told them this as not wanting to give my poor dad a heart attack on the spot, with telling him really that Relik was the new love of my life. Everyone relaxed a little and said hello to him. Relik, shook Dad's hand. "Very nice to meet you, sir." My dad looked surprised.

Visiting times were now nearly over, my parents and Donna were sleeping at my gran's place. But they reassured me they would be back early in the morning to see me. The moment they had gone including Gran, Relik pulled up a chair closer to me. He lent his face down on the pillow next to mine.

"I thought for sure you were dead and didn't know if I would be able to cope with that," he said sounding all choked up.

"I thought for sure I was a goner too. But amazingly I pulled through. But one of us didn't make it."

Relik was quiet, "So… you were pregnant then and you lost the baby?"

"Yes, I was not still even used to the idea yet. But I had decided to go ahead with the pregnancy. After all it was a new life and part of me. It didn't matter how it came to be," I said as a tear ran down my face.

"You're so amazing do you know that? Other people may not have the same beliefs or be able to stick to them so well in your situation. You treasure all life, which is such a beautiful quality about you. Along with so many other special things that make you who you are. That's the reason why I love you so much."

We looked at each other tenderly before our mouths finally met and we had our first kiss. Not exactly how I'd first imagined a first kiss would be. But it was still amazing all the less.

I slept surprisingly well, drugged up on some strong pain meds. I was unaware that Relik was standing guard at the front of the hospital the entire night. He was terrified Aluna would come back and try to kill her again. But he really needed to talk with the snails, to find out how to take her over in the body she was now in. Thankfully back up had arrived, in the nick of time. Two men slowly approached Relik, he sensed straight off that they were also Kachinas. He then discovered they had been sent by sanctuary to try and help. It unfortunately turned out Aluna, just like Sion feared, had swapped bodies yet again. The innocent guy she had taken over to stab me and Relik with, was now also dead. She had run in front of a police car deliberately wanting that body to die, after they were on her tail. She had located a Kachina in another body. It would be harder now to recognize her coming from a distance. As an extra precaution, for the time being there was a ban on any more swaps with humans. They also were going to try and bring back all the Kachinas already out there and get them to return

Relik came to see me the minute t visiting hours had started the next morning. He spent a while with me, just talking and kissing whenever the nurses weren't looking.

It felt so good to have him with me. It didn't faze me either that he was in another body. It proved to me that you loved someone for who they were inside, not out. But that wasn't to say the body he was now in wasn't hot, in fact he was darn steaming hot even. We didn't talk about the fact we did not know how long we had with each again. But it crept into my mind every so often. Mostly we talked about all my good experiences back in Sanctuary.

I said to him I never got close to the volcano of life. He informed me I was not permitted to, that it was a private experience only for other Kachinas. I was quiet in my thoughts for a while till more curiosity got the better of me. I asked him what coming together was like and which was better, Kachina or human. But I'd felt myself suddenly blush as I'd asked him this. Relik chuckled. "I have no idea, Gemma, I have yet to experience either of them."

I felt shocked and asked him how many times had he been a swap for a human? "This body I am now in, would make it only my third time."

"Really! So, the second time as Russell you get to experience being a human, it's to save my sorry arse."

He kissed me his plump lips pressed hard on mine. Releasing them he looked deep into my eyes. "But I wouldn't have it any other way." I looked at his eyes they were like a window to his soul and I also thought wow this body he was in had very long eye lashes.

After he had stayed a little longer, he said he was sorry, but he needed to go for a while. But he promised me he'd be back later. I told him he better I'd be waiting and missing him. But I knew my mum and dad would be up to see me soon, so guessed it was for the best he went.

On his way out the hospital car park he checked that the other Kachinas would keep guard till he returned. They assured him not to worry they would.

Chapter Seventeen

Relik waited till he had seen my mum, Donna and Dad leave grans place. Then he knocked on the front door. Gran invited him to come in and made him some breakfast. They talked for a while and Relik informed her of all the latest and with the plans they had. Gran said hopefully the snails would be willing to help him. So, when they were done eating they went out into the garden. Looking for snails sometimes could take a while, especially if they did not want to be found. But luckily Relik quickly spotted one hiding under a bush and it wasn't just a common snail. "Your plan, Relik, is a very foolish and dangerous one. Have you considered what may happen to you?" it said before Relik could even speak.

"Yes, but I see no other way unless you can tell me of one," he replied.

"I will need to consult a little more with the others, come back later tonight," the snail told him. With that the snail suddenly retreated quickly back inside its shell. Relik rose to his feet. Gran was sitting waiting for him, on the little metal bench next to the pond feeding the fish.

"Well, did it help you, Relik?"

"It wants to consult more with the others, it told me to come back later."

"Oh…ok. Well that's not a bad thing, it could mean they are seriously considering it. Have you told Gemma, anything yet about Aluna, and your plan?"

"No, not yet as I don't want her to be worried about me, not when she needs her strength to heal from her injuries."

Gran nodded but said. "You can't keep it long from her, she does deserve to know. Especially as Aluna, is still such a grave danger to her."

Relik sighed and looked sad down at the ground. "I know, but I will make sure she is safe whatever the cost maybe! Though I will tell her soon about everything. I don't want to hide things from her. "

Gran hugged him, well at least his waist as he towered above her.

He then returned to me in the hospital, just minutes after my parents and Donna had left again. I'd missed him so much and knew that our time together was so precious. Some more kissing was in order, even though that got us a few disapproving looks. I really hated being stuck in here, but with these injuries I knew I had no choice.

A nurse came over to me. "Gemma, I was asked to see if you needed to see someone to maybe talk to after your loss and the trauma. I'm guessing from looks of things this must be your partner, he can have counselling if he needs some too?" she said.

I wondered for a minute what she meant, then I suddenly realized. "Oh, no I will be okay, thank you and he was not my baby's father."

I suddenly cringed. God what a slut she must think I am I thought to myself. Especially as she looked embarrassed and apologized before going quickly to attend to another patient.

Relik smiled. "I'd better get going, Gemma, but I'll see you in the morning my love."

"I love you," I said smiling up at him.

He smiled his eyes twinkling back, "I love you too, now you get some rest." He kissed me passionately, smiled again and slowly walked away.

As Relik left the hospital, he chatted to my two special guards. Suddenly, one of them started looking anxiously around. He told Relik he sensed a presence. Immediately Relik also picked it up too.

They scanned the area, walking down a pathway at the side of the hospital was a tall black man wearing a hooded brown jacket. He was trying hard not to glance over in their direction, but his face looked angry. Relik and the others went straight for her, but she ran quickly off in another direction. They made chase, but she somehow managed to lose them. Relik concentrated hard, his connection with her of course was the strongest with her being his twin. After a few moments, he realized he could no longer detect anything. She must have got too much distance between them. This really alarmed him, he needed to talk to the snails. Though in truth, he did not want to leave me, not with me now under more threat. He knew the knowledge he could gain from the snails, would put an end to this once and for all. The others told him they would be extra vigilant tonight. That he must go he did not have a choice.

Reluctantly he left, saying he would be back as soon as he could. He got to Gran's place, but it was late, so he was not sure whether to knock on the door or to just creep through into the back garden.

Gran had been keeping an eye out for him to return and opened the front door. She told him whispering, it was safe to come through the house as everyone else had already gone to bed. He seemed agitated, so Gran asked him what was wrong. He told her everything that had happened with Aluna. His voice etched in fear.

"I really hope the snails help us, or I just might have to make snail soup out of them," Gran spat!

Relik grinned and followed her to the garden. Luckily, they didn't have long to wait till one arrived. Somehow Gran knew this one wasn't the same one which had spoken to Relik earlier on today. "We really don't taste good, you stupid woman. You'd also be very ill advised to even try something like that." It laughed but in a nasty sort of tone.

"Please you must help us, so many have died and the word may spread around. Then no one will ever want to use a Kachina again, not if it means they may not ever return or worse still, their body could be killed. This is much bigger than just Gemma's and my own life at stake," Relik pleaded.

"Well luckily for you, there are others of us that agree with you. I though myself couldn't really care less either way. You are all, even you Kachina's such mere life forms in comparison to us. But as I just said, you're fortunate the others do feel the need to help more disadvantaged beings and keep the balance." It replied, its tone sounding somewhat arrogant.

"So, what do I need to know? For me to be able to throw Aluna out of a body?" Relik asked now impatient. All he wanted to do was get back to the hospital. Not have it out with some slimy Mollusk, who had a serious superiority complex.

"Quite simple to be honest with you. That you will probably kick yourself, for being so unbelievably stupid, you had not realized it already for yourself. All you need is to use your strongest emotions. Be that revenge, love or hate, whatever ones you can home in on and use as a weapon. It just needs to be a much stronger emotion than theirs. Which I'd personally say, would mean you're pretty much screwed! As vengeance is one of the most powerful emotions there is," Relik screeched out loud, seriously pissed off. "That's all I need to do? That was all you needed to inform me of?"

"Yep that's it in a nutshell, didn't I just tell you that you would want to kick yourself," it replied conceitedly. Relik's face was mad, he turned saying to gran he must go, as he ran off jumping fast straight over the garden gate in a single leap. Gran frowned down at the snail.

"What? It's all their stupid fault any of this came to be anyway. Give me some slack, old woman, I did not have to reveal anything to him. It's not like I personally would have suffered any sleepless nights for not helping out you dimwits anyway," the snail said smirking as it slid slowly off.

Crunch! suddenly went its hard shell.

"Well, I certainly won't be having any sleepless nights for that either." Gran chuckled as she walked back off into the house.

Relik returned to the hospital. The two Kachinas told him there had been no more trouble. They asked if he had got all the knowledge he needed. He told them he had. All he needed to do now was to get out of this body he was still in. But he wasn't ready quite yet, he wanted to spend some more time with me first. Hopefully Aluna would not try again so soon, he'd thought to himself.

He took over as guard, so the others could go and get some rest. But moments later Relik heard a commotion going on in the next street over. Looking around, he raced fast around the corner. There he saw the two Kachinas and Aluna still inside the black guy's body fiercely fighting. Aluna had a weapon one of the Kachinas were holding tight onto her waist as the other one was trying to pry the carving knife out of her hand. Relik ran quick over and helped restrain her. One of the Kachina's face was deeply slashed as she tried desperately to fight them off. But with Relik holding her arm back tightly, the other one managed to get her to release the knife.

Aluna spit t hard into Relik's face. "You have no idea, Relik, of how I will make her suffer terribly for what you have all done to me," she screamed, full of pure hatred.

Relik tried hard to not let her words get the better of him as he grabbed her face. Squeezing it he looked deep into her wide eyes. "Have no fear, my sister, you will not ever have the chance to get close to her again. You will also pay severely for everyone you have harmed or killed. It will soon be over," he replied, his face wild with pure rage.

Aluna started to laugh loudly in an insane sort of way. "You stupid fool, what did you think I was acting alone? That I did not have some extra help? I have had help from where you idiots would have least expected it to come from too. You see, bro, there are other much more enlightened entities than us. Ones which don't like existing beside such mere animals, as they like to often call humans," she cackled.

Relik's thoughts returned to the arrogant snail, the one he had just encountered. Surely not, he worriedly thought to himself.

Aluna started to laugh again looking at his concerned reaction. But then she started foaming at the mouth, the body she was in slumped going limp into the other Kachina's arms. Quickly they pulled her up and between them lifted her and raced fast towards the hospital entrance. But it was too late, the body she had just been in was already dead. She had no intentions of ever being caught and had secretly carried inside her mouth a tiny vile of deadly poison. She had broken it with her teeth, when she had realized she was trapped. Now she was free yet again to be able to find another new body and take it over. The body count was mounting right up and Relik felt distraught. Him and the other Kachinas all kept guard that night, interrogating anything that dared move in the darkness.

Chapter Eighteen

Next day I was feeling good. Still sore, but I was healing very nicely the doctor said after examining me. You should be home for the weekend hopefully he told me, which was music to my ears. Although Mum wanted to stay with Gran to help get me back on my feet. So, it could prove difficult having some precious alone time with Relik. But I was still glad for her to stay, a bit of TLC couldn't really go amiss and I'd missed her too.

Relik was up the next morning to see me and we embraced each other. I felt though there was something bothering him. I was about to ask him, when he strangely started to fade in and out, becoming sort of transparent. He was horrified and said Scott wanted his body back, he was calling for Relik to return to sanctuary. "No, no you can't go yet, please don't go yet, Relik? Please stay here with me!" I watched him fade more away. He looked upset and his last words were, I love you, then he was gone.

I cried for hours, five years now until I would see him again. It did not bear thinking about. I was in an emotional mess when Mum and Dad later came up to visit.

Mum tried hard to get me to talk, but I just couldn't. Plus, there was no way they would believe any of it. So, I just sobbed pitifully on her shoulder.

Back on the beach of transition, Relik tried to convince Scott to give him more time. That he would understand everything, when he returned and installed the memories of everything which had happened. Scott was somewhat unsure, until Valla came and helped. She said Scott could trust Relik to return and this could help everyone here too. Scott finally agreed to let him have a little longer.

At my hospital bed Mum was sitting in a chair next me, Dad was standing and arguing yet again with Donna about how much make up she was wearing. She told him in her sarcastic tone, it was in the hope of picking up a hunky student doctor here. Which made my dad even more annoyed.

But suddenly I nearly shot up fifty feet into the air as I gasped out loud. Dad swung round fast to be nearly nose to nose with Relik and stepped quickly backwards. "Where the hell did you appear from?"

"Out of thin air actually," he replied smiling.

Dad looked pissed. "Oh, you think you're funny do ya? If you're the reason she's upset, you are not welcome here!"

Relik shuffled on his feet looking down at the floor before looking my dad in the eye. "I do believe, sir, I am the reason she is hurt. That's why I have come back. Believe me when I say, I am truly sorry for her distress and would never ever hurt her on purpose."

There was an awkward silence as dad glared at him. "Dad, can you give us some privacy please? We need to talk. I'll be okay I promise," I said with my puppy dog eyes look. Dad did not look happy as he gave Relik a stern look, as if to say hurt my girl again and I'll bloody kill you.

Mum got up and kissed me. "We will be in the hospital café, sweetheart, having a quick coffee, we won't be long." She pulled Dad by his arm. Donna scowled at Relik as she walked slowly past him. The moment they were all out of sight, I opened my arms out for him to hold me. I held on to him tightly as he held me close to his chest.

After a few more precious minutes, I slowly released my grip looking into his teary eyes. "Does this mean that you're a stealer now, Relik?"

"No definitely not, Gemma! I just asked Scott to allow me a little longer here with you."

He smiled as he lightly touched my cheek with the back of his hand. I was not sure how I felt about this, part of me was so glad he had not become a stealer because of me. But another part of me knew we were still in the same hopeless situation, that would cause us to be apart. Pushing them thoughts though quickly away, I pulled him close to me and kissed his sweet plump lips. Whatever time we had we really needed to make it count.

Chapter Nineteen

There was no sign of Aluna, and I was still unaware of anything that had recently happened. Along too of course with Relik's ultimate plan. A few more days passed and he wanted to talk to my gran alone, but there never seemed to be a right moment. Relik as usual was at the hospital visiting me daily, my mum and dad had concluded especially after the other day, that we were obviously more than just good friends. Dad did not approve of course, he thought that it was too soon with everything that I'd been through. Not to mention Dad even though not a feeble kind of guy, he still felt intimidated by Relik's hulking size. But he was willing to be tolerate towards him, after I'd begged him enough times. I could always get my way with my dad, just the words, but you know I love you Dad, normally worked.

Mum seemed to think maybe this was the breakthrough I needed. She said it proved there could be life after what I'd lost. I didn't have the heart to tell them, this could affect me worse in the long run. Not to mention, what I'd already lost. I couldn't consider telling them about the baby. But I hated keeping secrets from them, especially my mum.

Finally, the doctors let me leave hospital and go back to my gran's place. But only with strict instructions of lots of rest and relaxing. I could do that easily if I was with Relik, I thought smiling to myself. Dad and Donna needed to return home, so after settling me in and spending an hour or so with me they left. Mum was staying a few more days, she'd had terrible nightmares of how close she'd been to losing me. She was going to guarantee I listened to the doctor's advice, knowing I could be stubborn when it came to taking orders. So, I was lucky if she would even let me go the toilet alone. Though I did appreciate the help and love, it was not easy convincing her I was fine to be left alone with Relik. Mum made sure we both knew she was only in the other room. I rolled my eyes at her, what did she think I was going to rip off his clothes and pounce on him the minute we were alone. Although the thought soon crossed my mind, especially after things got a little heated up.

Relik pulled himself away a few times, especially as with what was going in his trousers. This was a completely new experience to him and he was finding his sudden urges, a little hard to keep under control. Made worse by the fact, that I'd said give me a few more days' recovery and you'll be getting your first experience of it. We could hardy keep our hands off each other and with the clock always ticking made it even more difficult. I still sensed Relik was holding something back from me. From time to time, I saw his face tinted with genuine worry. Of course, he assured me repeatedly there was nothing the matter.

Three days later my mum was happier with how I was doing. She finally said she better get back home and save my dad from killing Donna. But both her and Dad would be back up to see me early next week. She tried to convince me to come back home with her. But I told her I really wanted to stay longer. She wasn't stupid, she knew why as she looked smiling over in Relik's direction. We had our teary goodbyes and Uncle Rob drove her back home.

Gran had seemed a bit on edge lately too, I'd asked her what was wrong on a few occasions but kept on getting the same old response. Being, don't fuss or worry yourself there is nothing wrong, that she was just old and tired. But I knew deep down, there was something not right with the both of them.

One evening Gran went outside, I had a strong feeling it was to chat to the slimy nasty snails. Relik had not turned up to see me yet, which was also worrying me, so I slowly secretly followed her outside. Gran acted nervous, as she checked around bushes and rocks like she was looking for one. Which was unusual for her to be like this, she had never showed any fear of them before. I kept well hidden behind a large bush.

Suddenly, I felt someone put their arms gently around me. I quickly turned to see Relik. "Just what do you think you're doing out here, young lady? What would your poor mother say?" He smiled.

"Err nothing, I just wanted to get some fresh air." I lied hoping he'd believe it as I quickly kissed him.

"Where is your gran? I was wanting to talk to her about something," he said between kissing me back.

"She is err… here in the garden somewhere I believe."

The kissing increased to a more passionate level. But we were interrupted, when we heard someone arguing. It was Gran and she was having a heated conversation. Carefully holding onto Relik, we went slowly over to investigate. Gran was further up next to the stone rockery, there were three snails sitting on top of it. I heard something from Gran, about how the obnoxious so and so bloody deserved it. That everyone was equal in her eyes. That he had no right to act so dam high and mighty. A snail replied that did my gran not believe he would seek revenge for this. After all she had very inconvenienced him. Getting a new, flesh body took some serious energy for a nature sprite.

"Well I still don't care, and he better not dare ever show up here again, or I'll do exactly the same again," she warned them.

The main snail talking said that the snail in question had requested that no more council should be given to her from them. That she should not receive any help from the other spiritual beings either. He believed he had the right to have her banished without a trial from the Enlightened circle.

Gran quickly voiced she still believed she was justified in crushing the little arrogant arsehole.

Relik's eyebrows suddenly rose. I looked at him with deep suspicion. Something had gone down and as bloody usual, I was going to be the last one to know. We went to Gran, she looked at me as if she was sorry about something.

The main snail spoke again. "But we have decided he did in fact have it coming, he has always been far too big headed and needed bring down a notch or two. So, we denied his request. But you are on a severe warning to not ever repeat the incident, or anything similar. Otherwise we will have no choice but to end your membership in the circle," it sternly told her.

Gran thanked them all saying that she would do her best to control her urges to flatten him if he did cross her path again.

She then turned to me. "You should be resting, sweetheart, let's get you back inside, but there are things that you need to know. Relik you can't keep it from her any longer!" I looked at Relik, I did not like the sound of this.

We went back inside. Gran said I needed to get more comfortable, so she got yet another pillow for me and plumped it up. I felt concerned as I waited, becoming impatient for them to clue me in. Finally, Relik kneeled next to the chair I was sitting in. He took hold of my hand kissing it. "I really wanted to tell you before Gemma, but I wanted us to enjoy the time we have together without having to worry about what could happen or not.

"Relik, this is starting to scare me, please what is it, tell me?"

He hesitated. "When the body of the dying woman died, the one we fooled Aluna into, she should have been trapped in the dark place back in sanctuary. But instead of her being pulled straight into it, she somehow resisted and got away. Unfortunately, she escaped back to this dimension and took over the body Jaydin was inhabiting. Thus, destroying Jaydin." He looked sad staring at the ground.

I gasped. "Oh my god! No, Relik, that is dreadful."

I realized there was much more he needed to reveal to me, as he nervously gulped. "Since then Jaydin has not been the only one she has taken out in a swap body. She has killed more bodies that she had gained access into, each time finding another Kachina to throw out. The person who stabbed you and Russell's body, was in fact Aluna! He paused. "I have to be the one to stop her, Gemma, I may be the only one who really can."

"What are you going to do? Please don't say you're going to take her to the dark place like your first plan, are you?" I said terrified of what his response was going to be.

"No, not exactly, Gemma. But I have needed to learn what it takes to be a stealer. But only temporarily, I don't want to become one. The plan is for me to forcibly remove her from a body, eradicating her life force forever."

It took me a few minutes to register what he meant, but I realized this could seriously back fire. "But if you don't succeed, Relik, she will throw you out and you will be the one gone!" I cried.

"There is no other possible option, my darling, she must be stopped at whatever cost. She is intent on destroying as many of us as she can, anyone who she feels is responsible for tricking her into the dying woman's body. That includes you too and she tried to get to you again twice at the hospital. One time we managed to scare her off. Then another time she tried again just the night before you came back here. This time we all got into a fight and she killed the body she was in yet again so she could escape. She is intent on succeeding and killing you." He pulled me close to him, as if the very thought of it completely terrified him. I hugged him tightly back. I could not believe the mess this had all become. It was so dam unfair.

I asked him when this plan was meant to take place, he told me soon as she turns back up here. As most Kachinas had now returned to Sanctuary by orders of the Elders she would have difficulties in obtaining host bodies. So, she may bide her time and come up with a plan.

I knew we needed to try and make the most of this time. That we could waste no time. I told Relik, looking deep into his eyes, I wanted him to stay here with me tonight. He understood what I was implying but paused before answering, "You are still recovering from your injures, Gemma, I am not sure if you are physically up to something like that yet."

"Don't worry, I will be gentle with you. I do feel really good like I keep on telling you and Gran" I smiled.

Gran walked in, hearing that last bit. "Probably the reason for that, is the healing herb tea that the gnomes gave me for you." She smiled.

"Really! I wondered why the tea you keep giving me, tastes a bit funky." I smiled back up at her.

"It is good to have friends sometimes in high places. They saved your uncle's life when he was a child. Amazing what a few herbs can do."

I looked over at Relik, he gave me a wink. I took this to be a yes, I'll stay. Good job too, as I wasn't going to be taking no for an answer.

Relik said he needed to talk to my gran. She came over and sat down in a chair next to us. He began telling her about what Aluna had said to him, about help from other enlightened entities. That how he personally suspected it was the same snail my gran had smashed up. But he had wanted to talk to her first and see what she thought before he confronted them about it.

Gran's face changed to a look of horror, as he spoke. She would need to consult quickly with the Enlightened circle on this matter. She got up and went back out into the garden, she told us not to come, getting to talk with the Enlightened circle would not be permitted to us. It had taken her nearly her lifetime to be granted such a privilege.

We waited nervously for her to return. Relik was pacing up and down the brown patterned carpet. About two or so hours later she finally walked back in, but she did not look happy. We both stared at her. Gran said that she was so sorry it was true, it really was that arrogant snail. He in fact had been helping Aluna from the very beginning.

"Relik please sit down for what I must tell you." Relik looked at me apprehensive as he sat next to me on the sofa. Basically, it boiled down to this, the first swap she did unknown to her was with a very powerful, dark witch who gave her false memories of who she was. The witch was well informed of dealings in the Enlightened circle. When she made the swap with Aluna, she had no intention already of ever returning to her body. Poor Aluna suffered terribly as she tried in vain for years to discover a way of being able to return back to you. Gran told him how they said sometimes Aluna would listen to the wind blowing, as if she was lucky she could listen into Sanctuary and Relik calling to her. Relik had once told me over the years he would often try to send his love and support over to her through the beach of transition. Knowing wind could sometimes pick up on transmissions from other dimensions Gran told him she had even tried to drown the body she was trapped in, so that she could return to you and Sanctuary. She had jumped off a seaside pier and into the water, even though she knew this was forbidden by her kind to harm the host body. She only failed because she was saved by a couple of stealers. Ones who had pretended to just be Kachinas and befriend her, when all along they were working for the little shit snail.

Relik at this news broke down and cried, I held him close to me. Gran carried on telling us more and apologized for causing Relik such pain.

After years of trying everything, it finally dawned on Aluna she was trapped, so she tried to make the most of it. But unknown to her at the time, that snake in the grass was using all his negative influences on her. Including using the other stealers she thought were helping her, to convince her she was already not welcome back in Sanctuary after trying to kill her host body. Over time she dramatically changed, becoming so corrupted to the way she is now. The snail revealing himself to her when he believed she was ready, gave her all the knowledge how to be the most powerful stealer, so she would be able to resist the pull of the dark place. He also told her how to survive outside a host body for much longer than any other could.

Relik stood up with rage burning in his face and demanded to know why? Why would this nature sprite do such a terrible thing as this?

"That is probably the worst part about. He did this all only just because he wanted to see if he could. He was curious to see what the outcome would be and enjoyed the power boast he got from it. Although the rest of the Enlightened Circle suspect he really had higher motives, but he would not reveal them."

Relik, looked as if he had been punched hard in the gut. After he pulled himself back together. His expression was nothing but loathing for that sprite, something I'd never witnessed from him before. "What has become of this evil sprite, with all this information coming to light," he demanded angrily to know.

But before Gran could reply, he stormed out into the garden. Gran took me by the arm and led me gently out after him. He screamed out loud in the garden, that someone needed to tell him right now what punishment this snail, sprite or whatever it bloody was, would receive. No one however high and mighty they believed themselves to be, had the right to cause such suffering and loss of lives.

Everything was dead quiet, and I felt like I was holding my breath as we waited. "He no longer exists any more, Relik," came back the reply, sounding like it was from someone of great authority.

"How do I know this is to be true!"

"You don't, Relik! You will have to trust me that I am not lying. But I do give you my word this is the case. The sprite in question showed us his true colours, when his earthly body was destroyed. Then with other evidence which was mounting up against him, all this came to light. We could not allow such a being to be able to exist, we have rules we do take very seriously. From nearly the beginning of time, it has been the enlightened circle, who made it possible that Kachinas couldn't get into the human's realm without the swap ritual taking place after the stealers came into existence. That sprite misused his power and knowledge and we sincerely apologize, as this is not our way. We will grant you a portal when you go back to Sanctuary, to be able to return here in your non-corporal form and regrettably deal with your sister. As justice for what has been done."

Relik bowed his head, knowing this was something at least. But there was still the painful fact he must still destroy his own sister.

All was quiet, whatever had answered Relik, had left. I sat with him out there for a while, as tears rolled down his cheeks just hugging him. "I am so glad I have you,

Gemma, you are the light in this darkness that is burning inside me. I love you more than anything." He kissed me.

"I feel the same, Relik, now and for always," caressing his face with my hand.

Gran went to bed early She seemed exhausted by everything. I got up taking Relik by the hand and led him back inside. In the bedroom I lay down, he lay down next to me. He took me in his arms and kissed me with such a longing it was overwhelming that it took my breath away. Gradually our clothes started to come off. Other than my bandage, we were completely naked. I felt the intense desire burning from within our very souls. Though as things heated up, I noticed there was something strange happening. Relik started feeling not as solid. I stopped abruptly and opened my closed eyes. He was fading again. "No not again!" I screamed. "Why now of all the times? Refuse to leave just yet, Relik, please!" I begged. I could see the pain again in his eyes. "You can't leave me all alone it is not safe! Aluna is after me, remember?" I cried out.

"Sion and the others are going to look out for you in my absence. I would never leave you otherwise. But I must go now, I love you always," he replied as he completely faded away.

Chapter Twenty

I lay there naked in shock, pain intoxicating my soul. I couldn't breathe, I felt like my heart was on fire and it would turn to a burnt ash. But I knew I could not let myself go completely to pieces, I had to cling on to whatever fragment of strength which remained. I had to say strong for my Relik and with what he intended to do. I knew I owed it to him and our love.

Back at Sanctuary after Relik had given Scott all the memories of what had happened here, he made the swap. A naked Scott was returned to his neighbour's back garden, in the fairy ring he'd discovered some weeks ago. Lucky for him it was night time and the neighbours were all sleeping, as he jumped quickly over the fence. But he realized he had another problem, his house keys and everything had been in his trousers. This was going to be very interesting, he thought to himself. He remembered his good friend Jack down the road had a spare key. But this still meant he'd have to creep naked down the whole street. He cursed Relik's name the entire way there. Especially when another neighbour a guy he knew, was laughing out his bedroom window at him as he passed trying to cover up his private parts.

Relik on his return to Sanctuary went straight to the lake of dreams for a while. He needed to heal some pain and get rest for the battle that lay ahead of him. His thoughts were only of me as he slowly sunk deep down into magical lake

In the morning when I woke up I felt a stab of pain in my heart, with not having Relik waking up next to me as planned. I was not sure how I was going to get through the day or any other one without worrying to death about him. I knew I would find it hard to concentrate on anything other than wondering what was going on between him and Aluna. I leaned down and slowly picked up the clothes from off the bedroom floor. The ones Relik had last been wearing. I could not believe we had been so close to consummating our relationship. Of all the times he would get called away did it really have to have been right at that moment. It made me wonder if there were other bad forces out there, intent on making us suffer as much as possible. Like we had broken some sacred vow in falling in love and the powers that be wanted to come between us as much as they could.

As I was angrily folding up the trousers, a wallet and the keys fell out. Oh dear! That could be a problem I thought to myself. Opening the wallet, I looked for something with Scott, his host body's address or anything. Luckily as not many of us do it, he had filled in his home address on the card which came with the wallet. It was in London, so I figured I'd just have to get the train there and take it and the bag of clothes that Relik had borrowed to him personally. It was the least I could do, especially with him letting Relik have a little extra time with his body. But again, I really wished his timing had been a bit better. I decided not to tell my gran, I knew she would put up some resistance to me going. Primarily because it was so soon from coming out of hospital. But that magic herb tea was amazing, I felt completely rejuvenated. Gran really needed to get that into retail, she'd make an absolute fortune. Although something told me the enlightened circle would have objections to that.

Creeping out the house was not an easy task, I'd nearly got caught. I waited patiently till Gran had finally dozed off in her comfy chair, just as she normally always did most afternoons. I left her a quick note explaining what I was doing, and tiptoed gently down the hallway to the door. But as I opened the front door it creaked, and I heard her slightly stir. I peeked nervously around the living room door, but luckily, she had gone straight back off.

The train trip down there was uneventful and I got a taxi then straight to Scott's place. I thought he wasn't in after ringing the doorbell a few times, but finally it opened, and he stood there dripping wet with a towel wrapped around his waist. Oh, my bloody god! I thought to myself. I'd not thought this one out well. Scott stood there half naked wet and looking all gorgeous was just how I'd last seen Relik. It made this all pretty awkward to say the least. "Gemma!"

I jumped backwards as it took me by surprise he'd recognized me. But I stupidly remembered of course he would, he would have been given all the memories from Relik.

At least he hadn't had the terrible shock of discovering he was pregnant by a one-night stand though. I cringed thinking about what Valla may have got up to wearing my meat. But Relik was gonna use Scott's body too, so really, I was being a hypocrite.

Scott in the meantime looked a bit uneasy. "Please come in, Gemma, make yourself at home."

I shook my head. "That's okay I just wanted to return your things, the clothes, wallet etc," I said blushing, as it occurred to me he would have the memories that we were going to have sex with his body. "Gemma, you have come a long way and you only just got out the hospital. I have to insist you rest and a maybe a hot drink or something. Your gran would be very unimpressed with me otherwise," he replied just as I would have expected Relik to have done.

I hesitated but agreed it may be a good idea. Although Gran's tea had been a godsend, I was probably due another dose by now. It was beginning to wear off I reckoned as a bad pain seared right though the upper part of my abdomen. Scott apologized for all the mess, as he quickly cleared some stuff off a chair for me. I sat gently easing myself down into the old looking leather chair, opposite a small blue sofa. Scott went to throw some clothes on and make a coffee. It was good he was covering up, I'd felt uncomfortable looking at his hot, muscular body and trying desperately not to think of him as Relik.

I looked around the room, it was a small living room, but then again, the whole house was. London house prices were terrible, but I hoped to live here one day. The walls were painted yellow and there was a cute little log fireplace. On the mantelpiece, it was full of dragon ornaments. The walls were bare no pictures or photos anywhere. I sat uncomfortably waiting for Scott to bring the coffee in. This was such a bizarre situation to be in. I imagined it was not easy for poor Scott either. After all, he would still have fresh memories too of seeing me completely naked. Wow this was more embarrassing by the moment I thought as my cheeks felt warm to the touch.

He poked his head around the corner of his kitchen. "Do you take sugar and milk in your coffee?"

"Yeah, one sugar and milk please," I smiled. "I am trying to cut down I have put some weight on lately.

"Oh, no with just seeing your figure it's perfect."

Now my cheeks felt on fire as I gave out an embarrassed giggle. Scott looked a little red faced too as he brushed his fingers through his hair. "Oops, so sorry, that just slipped out."

I grinned at him. "It's okay, I totally understand."

He smiled back and returned to the kitchen.

After a few more minutes Scott walked in and passed me a steaming mug of hot coffee. I thanked him as he sat on the chair. Our eyes met for a moment, but I quickly looked away. "I am not sure if this helps you, Gemma, but Relik does really love you very much. The memories of his feelings towards you are pretty intense," he told me, trying not to look into my eyes as he said it. That really pulled at my heart strings and I gulped hard, feeling the water building up behind my eyes. I wiped them with my sleeve and tried hard to not look upset.

"Does he really believe he can win and beat Aluna? Did you pick that off him by any chance?"

Scott shifted uncomfortably in his chair. He looked like he was thinking hard of what to say. It made me think straight off, that I already knew the answer myself.

After a moment, Scott replied Relik was going to go in guns blazing, that he would give it his best shot whatever it took. He had to make sure that you would be safe. But deep down, he was afraid he would fail and feared the consequences. But not for himself, but for you.

My tears were now no longer hiding in the corner of my eyes, they had made their way right down my cheeks. Scott got up grabbed some tissues from the nest of coffee tables in the corner of the room. He handed them to me and sat back down. "I'm so sorry, Gemma, part of me wanted to lie to you and say he had no doubt he would defeat her. But I do not want to give you false hope."

He rose from his chair, putting his hand comforting over mine and squeezing it gently. I slowly pulled away from him and said I must leave now, that Gran most likely would be going berserk with worrying about me. Scott nodded and said he understood. He looked sad though as I left through the front door. I paused turning and looking at him. "Can I ask you, that's if you don't mind, Scott, why you wanted a swap with a Kachina in the first place. What were you going through yourself that you needed to escape here for a while?"

Scott hesitated, then looking right at me, said that it was because he was so lonely, that he wanted to form a close meaningful relationship with someone. But he didn't seem to be able to make connections with people, women in particular very easily. So, he wanted a break for a bit from his loneliness.

"Oh!" was about all I could say to that. This must be even harder on him, I thought. Relik and me shared something so strong and he had all them memories to now contend with. I felt so guilty for Scott. I told him as I left out the steel garden gate. That I really hoped things worked out for him and that he met that special someone soon. He thanked me as he slowly closed the door.

Chapter Twenty-one

In Sanctuary Relik believed he was nearly ready to take Aluna out. But this was with a great amount of sorrow. They had shared a powerful bond together and the same essence of life. But he accepted, this was the only course of action that could be taken. A lot rested on him being able to fully shut of his emotions to the fact she had once meant so much to him. He needed to be prepared to extinguish her existence forever.

The other Kachinas were trying to prepare him for the journey over to our realm. It would be a different transition than he would normally make, as he would need to cross over in a non-corporeal body. But a Kachina had a short time of being able to survive in our realm without a physical body so he needed to find Aluna quickly. Stealers had somehow managed to cling onto their essence in our realm for much longer than Kachinas and with Aluna gaining help from the nature sprite, it was not known how long she could do this for. But the process of throwing her out would still always be fatal even for her.

After Elders had talked with the Enlightened Circle, the Circle revealed to them   that each time a stealer would overthrow a Kachina it would ingest a small part of the other one's essence of life. So, this was concerning, considering Aluna had already thrown out quite a few in such a short time. Meaning there was strong possibility she would be too powerful for Relik to overcome. Other Kachinas were trying to empower him with their own energy. A Kachina called Demarick had already gone over and made a swap in the hope of being able to locate Aluna quicker for Relik. He was now waiting for Demarick to return so he could leave and go ahead with this dreaded mission.

The train trip back to Gran's place, really made me think again about the whole thing surrounding swapping with a Kachina while you try and recover in Sanctuary, worries and cares seem to completely disappear. But it's when you return from your vacation to your not so great life, that things could seem even harder than they were before. I was beginning to wonder, if anyone ever actually had a successful swap which ended with a more positive outcome. There certainly should be a big health warning with having a swap, other than your body might get stolen. But then if I'd have known beforehand about all this stuff possibly happening, I might not have gone ahead and swapped, then I would never have met the special person who was now in my heart, my Relik.

Back at Grans place, I got all the disproving moans and groans from her that I had been expecting the moment I walked back in. I looked rough too, so that didn't help matters either. Gran quickly went and made some of the special herb tea and told me to drink it down quickly. After a while I felt like it was already working as the pain was eased, but not just physically but also a little mentally too. I really wanted to thank them Gnomes in person and not to mention maybe ask them for a lifetime supply.

But even the Gnome potion could not seem to help the sudden despair I sunk deep into a few days later. I was totally overcome in my grief for Relik and I hit an all-time low. How would I even know if he was okay and would I ever see him again. What if he was already dead and I didn't even know it. Is this how poor mothers felt when they had children go off to war. I started totally freaking out. Gran and Uncle Rob had been on the firing end of my bad attitude. But luckily my gran had found out the reason for my sudden despair, after a Merfairy had whispered something to her at the bottom of the garden. Unknowingly I was being fed some nasty negative energy by a Wakacuna. She'd witnessed the treacherous, squirrel cross, cat thing entering through the glass in my bedroom window last night. I believed I had a caught a glimpse of it once one night, when it had visited me in my room. I had suddenly felt as if I was being watched and swore I saw a little, dark shadow thing moving on the top of my wardrobe. I thought it was my wild imagination as usual getting the best of me. But I should have known better, being in this house.

My gran wasted no time and had raced up to my room in an instant of being told that morning. She quickly threw some red holly berries all around the room. She scared me half to death, as she loudly started chanting some incantation of sorts. I suddenly heard a horrid squeal coming from under my bed, as something black and furry scurried straight through the closed window. I was shocked and even more so that whatever it was it could pass right through the glass, as the pane was not broken it just gently shook.

"What the flipping heck was that, Gran?" I screamed out.

"It was a Wakacuna nasty little entity, it inhabits certain trees mainly sycamores. I know there are some sycamore trees a few streets away, so I always keep a holly bush in the garden. I then collect them in a jar when they are in season. The berries repel it with good energy, the little buggers love only negativity and will feed right off it. It was feeding you a little negative energy for nights without us knowing, so it could then harvest a larger amount off you in the near future," Gran replied as she scattered more berries on the bedroom floor and along the window sill.

"Will that really get rid of it, some bloody stupid berries?"

"No just keep it at bay, it won't stop till it gets the negativity back off you it so craves."

"So, I am guessing you know how to get rid of it completely?" I snapped.

"Oh yes, dear, we need to give the bad negative energy to an ancient Tree Nymph," she replied with what sounded to me in an aggravating tone, which really pissed me off. To me this all sounded like it was the most normal thing in the world, and everyone should already know about it.

"Okay, Gran, so just how do we do this exactly? What do I need to do eat bloody wood chips or something?" I asked as I folded my arms crossly. The effect of its negativity was making me such a cranky bitch.

"Get dressed, myself and your Uncle Rob will take you there." She then surprisingly squashed a few holly berries right on the top of my head.

"Oh, my god, Gran, why did you have to go and do that?" I screeched.

"It will help you, at least for a short time," she said smiling leaving my room.

What now? I angrily thought to myself, I have to go out with flipping squashed holly berries on my head. This all seemed so bloody ridiculous. But everything did right now. I could not concentrate and focus on anything positive.

I heard a scratching noise outside my window. I slowly crept forward but jumped right back as two, beady little yellow eyes, were staring at me. I made a quick exit near enough flying down the wooden, winding, stairs.

Uncle Rob was already here. He only lived a street away in a little one bed apartment above the local coffee shop. Uncle Rob tried hard not to smile seeing the berries squashed on my head, but I soon shot him an irritated look that he better pack it in. He rolled his eyes and walked out to the car.

We got to the same woods again, the one where I'd gone to have the swap. It wasn't really the place I wanted to be right now, it certainly wasn't helping me with any positive energy. We walked on but I often swore something small was following behind us. I would see something dark, dart quickly away in the corner of my eye.

Gran stopped walking. "Okay we're here this is it." She stopped in front of a very large old looking oak tree. I looked up at it, some of the branches were huge. It had an almost wise kind of appearance to it, but a little intimidating at the same time. Gran spoke out. "I ask the wise, old tree nymph who resides here inside this tree, to please help take away the negativity in my granddaughter and feed it back to the earth. So, the earth can dispel it harmlessly into the air."

I stood wondering what the hell was going to happen. Suddenly I saw an aura glow around the tree which grew brighter and brighter. In the middle of it I saw something move, it was ethereal in appearance. A face gradually appeared, like an old man's. "Get her to place her hand on the trunk of the tree, I will gladly remove it for her. But first, I must deal with the cause of her unnatural negativity," it replied in a strange echo voice. Suddenly a ghostly long arm shot out from the tree to a nearby bush. The bush started shaking violently and a horrid high-pitched scream could be heard. The arm shot back inside the tree taking the squealing, little, black demon along with it. I looked shocked by this, but it didn't seem to faze Gran at all, like she had been expecting it to happen. Gran took me closer to the tree and told me I needed to place my hand flat on the bark. That I must not let go till she told me to. I placed my hand on the tree and shut my eyes, as looking at the face was freaking me out. I felt an odd sensation like an electric current, go through my hand and straight into the tree. It could be described, as if all your nerve endings were like live wires.

Slowly, I started to feel less negative. Soon I was told by my gran to take my hand away, that it was done. Gran thanked the tree nymph for its help and we slowly walked away. As we carried on back out of the woods, I noticed there were other trees which also had a white aura surrounding them.

I looked at Gran as we kept on walking back to the car. "Do all the trees with white auras have tree nymphs?"

She nodded and took my hand in hers. "This wood is renowned for being a powerful source of mystical energy, one which sustains the tree nymph's life force. They are all connected with each other under the ground by their roots, which spread out to other trees with tree nymphs all over the country. But all trees are more alive than you can imagine, if you place your hand on them and you have the gift you can feel what they feel. I fear so much that one day, the wood will be cut down and made into yet another housing estate. This would be a tragedy to us all.

Back at my gran's place, I did feel better but still concerned for Relik. I'd apologized to Gran and Uncle Rob if I'd been an off with them. But they both had told me not to worry, they understood with the Wakacuna and everything which had happened recently, I was not myself. Gran said I'd been mild in comparison to when my Uncle Rob had been affected by one. He still had the scar on his nose from getting in a fist fight with someone he'd rubbed up the wrong way. He'd also spent a night in the cells at the local police station too. Gran had squashed a lot more holly berries on his head, to get him down to the woods.

Uncle Rob laughed out loud. "I think it may have been beneficial to my hair. I think having a berry shampoo may have prevented me from going bald."

I laughed. "I'll keep it in mind as a new craze for washing your hair."

A few days later Gran came up with a possible suggestion about how to help Relik. Also, maybe if I was lucky know the outcome. My eyebrows rose up. "What's that, Gran?"

"There is something called an Ion it is an oracle, a gentle shy being that has the ability to know things no one else possibly can. But successfully finding one could prove difficult, as they fear humans after being nearly hunted to extinction centuries ago.

"Why were they hunted?"

"Because of fear of anything different, ignorance of the unknown. It is such a shame that mankind is not more spiritually aware," she sadly replied.

"What do they look like, Gran?" I asked.

"They are short pale and hairless but have a humanoid appearance. To be honest providing they are wearing a hat you generally would not suspect they weren't," she said.

"What if they are not wearing a hat then?"

"You have heard the old saying, Gemma, about having eyes in the back of your head, haven't you?"

"Yes," I replied looking even more curiously at her.

"Well Ions have exactly that, two eyes at the back of their heads. But these are not normal seeing eyes. They are psychic ones, that see the unknown and at times see things to come," she said with a smile on her face.

"Let's go right now and try and find one, I feel so helpless stuck here doing nothing while poor Relik is risking everything," I replied suddenly full of hope.

"Yes, but as with a lot of things Gemma, there are often consequences."

"Like what?" I asked worriedly.

"Things which are not meant to be known, can sometimes change the future as it should really be. To balance one thing out, sometimes an Ion must take something away as a price," she replied sounding serious.

"Gran, I am just about willing to try anything right at this moment."

Gran sighed. "Okay we need to go down to the beach, they like to be near saltwater as they can't drink normal water. Hopefully we will get lucky, as I believe I once came across one many moons ago when I myself was a little girl."

We made our way to the beach, Gran reckoned if one was living in this area, it would hide in the caves on the cliff at the end of the beach. Plus of course she had another trick up her sleeve for locating one. In her hand, she held a small pouch made of blue velvet, inside from the smell of it was a bunch of lavender seeds. She told me that as we neared the caves she would sprinkle some, if one did live close by, it would change into a purple smoke that would lead us right to it. Low and behold it did exactly that as Gran released some seeds into the sea breeze. A purple smoke drifted off down the beach and we quickly followed it to a nearby cave. The smoke sped up as we entered and disappeared fast inside. The cave was dark and damp my feet sinking in a combination of wet sand and shells. As we got deeper in we could also smell what smelt strangely like bacon.

In the darkness, we suddenly heard a deep voice. "Please leave me alone, I do not want to have to cause any more pain. Too often the price can be hard to bear. I already know, Gemma, who you are and I fear deeply for what must be taken as a price," it said in a croaky sort of voice.

"Surely that should be my decision and mine alone," I replied.

There was an eerie silence, before we saw something shuffling in the darkness. It got closer till we could finally see what looked like to be a small hooded man. He was covered in the lavender seeds, which were now glowing. "This is why I hide from mankind, it's not just because of being hunted years ago, although that certainly sucked. But the main reason I do, is because of the terrible torment I suffer inside. You cannot imagine the burden I feel, for the misery which has been caused. All because of what I can do. But I guess I understand why people still need to go ahead with this. So, we should get this over and done with," he replied his face sad.

Gran looked concerned, as if maybe this was the wrong path to go down. The Ion removed his hood and turned around. Two closed eyes that were on the back of his bald head sprung open. I stepped back a little fearfully, but Gran took my hand and squeezed it. The eyes were inhuman looking, like cats' eyes and menacing. They were wide open and stared straight forward as in a bizarre trance.

After a few moments passed, he spoke again. "The price you must pay for the information you seek, is that someone else on your behalf will suffer great pain and misery because of your love for each other. Are you willing to accept this?"

I hesitated to respond and thought hard about what Relik would think of this. I knew deep down he would be horrified if someone else was to suffer pain because of us. Especially, as there had been a lot already caused to others by our situation. "How long do I have before I need to answer you?" I asked, looking over at Gran to see if she gave anything away in her face that I should do.

"I must ask for an immediate answer I'm afraid."

"Well, I guess the answer must be no! The cost is too high. Why can't I be the one to suffer instead?"

"Sorry, Gemma, but I don't make the rules, or decide what the price should be. I am just the messenger of this terrible curse if you like. If it was up to me, all people who I felt really deserved this help would have no price at all to pay. But this unfortunately is how it all works," he said turning back around and pulling his hat up over his freaky eyes.

"Well I guess we better be going then." I looked again over to Gran. "I thank you for your time and do hope people who know about this don't find you. So far, I have learnt the Enlightened circle are in fact cruel at times."

He nodded. "I would agree there with you, but a few are not so bad."

"Huh, well I am not so sure, although I did have a good massage from the Leprechauns but with a price too."

I stared at Gran "So I know the snails, Griffins and the leprechauns, I think dragons, are part of the circle but who else?"

"Yes, you're right, Gemma. As well there is the Tree Nymphs, the four elements Sprites, the Gnomes and the Giants."

"Oh, the gnomes too. Okay they have some good pain relief and helped me out. Guess they are not all bad."

The Ion smiled, I put my hand out to him, he took it and shook it. "It is a pleasure to meet you, Gemma."

"You also. Err... oh do you have a name?"

He grinned. "Yes of course, my name is Thomas."

"Very nice to meet you, Thomas," I smiled and released my hand.

Gran shook his hand too. "Yes, same here, Thomas, and thank you."

Gran locked arms with mine. "We better go and leave him in peace, Gemma." I nodded, and we began to leave the cave.

Thomas called me back. "Because you have decided not to be selfish and cause pain to another, there is something I wish to give you."

"Oh, okay," I said wondering what this could be.

He touched my forehead with two fingers, as he did a warm light shone from his hand and in a flash felt as if it went inside my head.

"What was that?" I asked shocked.

"You will know soon enough, go back home it will all become clear in time." He smiled.

We thanked him again as we left, I asked Gran if she had any idea what it could be that he gave me. But she didn't have a clue.

Back at Gran's place I tried to keep a look out for anything out of the ordinary, but nothing happened. It finally got late and I decided to go up to bed, maybe whatever it was it had not worked. I was soon fast asleep and had the most perfect dream. I was back in Sanctuary with Relik, we were embracing each other tenderly. The peace of being back with him felt overwhelming. Even though I was aware this was a dream I decided to kiss him, it was so passionate and felt remarkably like we had solid bodies. I was sure   if we had shared a kiss when I was in Sanctuary, it would   have felt just   like this. I told him how much I loved and missed him, he said he wished we could live in this dream how real it all felt. Agreeing I kissed him again, our desire for each other was explosive.

Suddenly our tails or whatever they were, locked strangely tight together. Relik moaned. "Oh, Gemma, this mating is forbidden, unless you are an elder," he said as an intense pleasure took hold throughout our bodies. We stayed locked together like that for a while, the pleasure indescribable. "As much as I want to stay in this dream forever, Gemma, I have to leave the Lake and prepare myself in fighting Aluna," he said as our tails broke free. I then suddenly woke up.

I lay there feeling so good, like my whole body was tingling from my head to my toes. Wow I thought to myself that was some awesome dream. I got up and went down to the kitchen to make some breakfast. Gran looked at me surprised and remarked how I had a strange, golden glow surrounding me . I went and looked in the living room mirror, shocked I saw she was right it was like a yellow aura was brightly radiating off my body. I rushed back to Gran asking if she had any idea what this could be.

"Maybe it is the gift the Ion gave you, anything strange you can think of happen in the night."

I blushed remembering my dream. But thinking about it all, was it really a dream? Maybe it was somehow real. I told Gran I had a very vivid dream, that I was back in Sanctuary with Relik. That we had shared a very personal experience together. Gran laughed loud saying, that must be it then and I had the afterglow from it. She laughed again saying it must have been one hell of coming together.

I looked again at my myself still glowing in the mirror. "You could say that," I replied smiling back.

Gradually as the day went on, the glow slowly diminished. I could not help wondering if Relik knew too that it was not just a dream. I was so grateful to the Ion.

The doorbell rang. "I will get it, Gran." I opened it. "Umm, Relik, err... I mean, Scott. What are you doing here?"

"I feel compelled to come and check on you that you're okay. It's like Relik is still a little part of me, I can't explain it to be honest."

I hesitated unsure what to do or think. Scott stared at me. "Okay please come in, Scott. I showed him into the living room.

Gran walked in holding a pile of ironed clothes which she nearly dropped on seeing him. "Gran, it's not Relik, it's Scott."

"Oh... yes I did think for a moment. Hello, Scott, please don't mind me, sit down and make yourself comfortable."

Something though in Gran's face showed she was worried about this.

Chapter Twenty-two

Relik still in Sanctuary had floated out of the lake, after the dream he and myself had shared. He believed it had also seemed too real, but either way he felt he'd been given an extra incentive to succeed.

Demerick had returned and he knew exactly where Aluna was, though he told Relik he needed to act fast. He believed I was in imminent danger. Relik become incredibly anxious at the news and the other Kachinas tried to calm him down, he needed to stay focused. A whirling portal like the nature sprite had promised him, suddenly opened on the beach of transition. Everyone wished him a safe journey and good luck. He then rose up and slipped fast through the gateway to my dimension. The particles which formed his ethereal body felt like they were being painfully dissected into the atmosphere. Just like if he was in a human body and it was being cut into tiny little pieces with him surviving through the whole horrific process. Relik was in agony passing through like this to our realm of existence. But there was one thing which kept him grounded and willing to endure this terrible torture without wishing for immediate death, and that thought was me!

Aluna was now in the body Sion had been a Kachina for. Poor Sion had died as usual in this procedure of been taken over. Aluna planned on getting quickly to me, hoping I would not suspect she wasn't actually Sion. Relik though already knew this terrible information from Demerick, he also knew roughly whereabouts she should be. Aluna was travelling on a bus packed full of passengers, it was heading near towards my gran's place. She was sitting on the bus with a sharp hunting knife tucked inside her handbag. She was determined to make sure she finished the job this time. She hated me so much she hardly thought of anything other than slowly and painfully gutting me like a pig and making sure I was dead this time. I was her number one on her most wanted list, then followed closely by Relik and Valla. She had destroyed the other ones she held responsible for her situation. But to her now all Kachinas were her enemy, she contemplated on whether or not she would ever stop trying to make any other Kachinas suffer too. She had started to think of getting other stealers to join up force with her. That maybe they could travel back to Sanctuary and release all the other stealers from the dark place. Together as a powerful team they could completely take Sanctuary out for good. But first things first, she wanted to concentrate all her energy on getting her personal revenge. So, for the moment she was only focused on me and would think more on them plans later. She was also glad she was back in a female body. Generally, Kachinas liked to only swap with their own gender. It was much easier to act and feel like that person they were in. Male bodies also grossed her out.

Suddenly Aluna started feeling uneasy, like if she was being followed or watched. She looked suspiciously around the bus. She sensed there were no other Kachinas on board with her. But she could not put her finger on it, as there was definitely something strange in the air. What she unknowingly was picking up, was Relik was flying close and unseen to her behind the bus. He was in his non-corporal form, that in this realm was like a small bright blue glowing mist. He was waiting for his chance to get into the body Aluna was in. He believed the time to do it was right now.

He entered quickly through the back window of the bus, locating Aluna immediately. She was shockingly aware it was his presence she had been picking up all along on. She guessed straight off what his intentions were and quickly stood up from the chair screaming at the top of her lungs for the bus driver to stop the bus. But it was too late.

Relik in a flash was inside with her and the fierce battle began. The body that Aluna and Relik was in, screamed out so loudly with such deafening squeals it near enough rocked the entire bus. She then started thrashing about, like the time Relik had drew her into Russell's body. But this time much more forcefully and ferocious.

Everyone had been right Aluna now possessed great strength. People onboard started screaming and crying as the body shook so unnaturally, throwing itself all around the bus. Its arms and legs were thrashing out hitting other passengers and its face was scarily contorted. Deafening inhuman noises erupted screeching from its deformed features. It all sounded like something in a horror movie. Some of the terrified passengers tried desperately to get up and out of the bus. The driver was trying frantically to pull over somewhere safe, as the sheer panic unfolded. But along with the horrendous scene being witnessed and the stampede of people trying to escape the bus it swerved and skidded crashing hard into a large van. The impact caused the bus to fall, turning on its side as it slid further down the road.

Things were dead quiet for a few minutes or so, then along with some people screaming the body the two were still fighting over, started violently shaking yet again. There were bodies of dead and injured people laying around them, along with broken glass and other wreckage. Relik inside the body was using his strongest emotion as a weapon against her, as he kept on trying to overcome and push her out. He was close, he felt, as he started to feel her life essence slowly slip away from this vessel. But he could not let his defenses down for a second, with any thoughts of sorrow for his sister or she could use this back against him. He focused hard on just thoughts of overpowering her and saving me.   He... won

He felt her life ebbing away, like a breeze of gentle wind as she left the body. He wretchedly sensed she no longer existed, other than a tiny fragment of her essence remained inside with him. Tears ran down the cheek of the woman he was now in. It was over she was defeated and his sister was no more. This body he was in was injured, but luckily not too badly. One of the arms felt broken and one leg had a deep cut along it. The face also had some deep bloody cuts and bruises on it. He felt so guilty though, as he looked at the bodies of people who had come off a lot worse. He hated innocent people being hurt, by something that was not their fight. But he knew he was helpless to be able to change the outcome.

He slowly got up, pushing some bus wreckage off his other leg and made his way out through one of the mangled bus's broken windows. He cut the good arm on the shards of glass, as he did crying out. A few other injured passengers who could also walk, quickly moved out of the way as soon as they saw him in the female body coming toward them. A look of fear and horror was haunting their shocked expressions, Relik tried hard to ignore them. He then heard the sirens blaring in the near distance, as he quickly limped turning the corner into my grans street. The two Kachinas that had been my personal security, were on guard outside Gran's place. They thought for a moment it was Sion as they rushed over to help her. But shocked they quickly learnt it was in fact Relik. There was much relief as it was all over now. But at the same time a great sorrow for the loss of their poor Sion.

Chapter Twenty-three

The doorbell rang, Gran went and answered it. Something made me suddenly pause, while I was talking with Scott like I somehow knew Relik was close by. The minute Gran called out my name, my instincts were confirmed, and I do think I flew to the front door as my feet hardly touched the floor. There standing there was a Kachina who repeated to me what they had just informed Gran of. The other Kachina held tight on to Relik in the body of the woman. I was taken back, but so overjoyed Aluna was finally gone and Relik was going to be okay. I had been praying for this day to come. They brought Relik in and helped him to lay down on the sofa. "We should get her, I mean him to the hospital quickly I think," said my gran.

"No, not yet," said Relik in a soft feminine voice. I just wanted to throw my arms around him and kiss him so bad. But I was not too comfortable with the female body he was in. I'd not thought about that happening, so this was seriously awkward. Especially made worse, when Scott with his huge, bulking manly body walked into the living room.

Gran had already gone outside and told him what was going on. Relik looked surprised to see Scott here. None of us at all, seemed very at ease with the odd situation we were now all in. After I cleared my thoughts and came to my senses, I went and hugged Relik tightly. I considered closing my eyes and kissing him but it seemed far too messed up. But I did tell him I loved him so much and had been going out of my mind with worry for him.

He looked over at Scott with a puzzled look and I got the feeling a little concerned too. Noticing this I brushed some long strands of blonde hair out of his face, as I told him Scott had just popped by to check how I was doing. He pulled me to him and held me close. But he could also tell the gender of the body he was now in made me feel unnerved. "I do understand, Gemma, you don't feel comfortable with me being in this body. I don't feel very at ease either myself. I intend to return this body back to its rightful owner very soon," Relik said.

"No, you only just got here, Relik, you can't go yet. Give me just a bit more time. I'll get used to it," I said trying to sound like it really would not be a problem.

Holding onto his hand, I heard a sound like someone clearing their voice. I looked over to where the sound came from, it was Scott. "I have a solution for this predicament, if you're both interested?" Relik's eyebrows rose with a look of interest of what he had to say. I asked Scott what his idea was?

"Use my body again, just for a while. I would not mind spending a bit more time back at Sanctuary I guess," But before I leaped at the very chance, Relik had already said no quite loudly without even the slightest pause for thought. I looked at him my face shocked. Why would he say no? I thought strangely to myself.

Relik went on to explain. "It is quite obvious that as Scott is here, he has formed a strong connection to you, because more than likely of the memories that I gave him. It would not be fair or right to then subject him to even more. It could all be very mentally damaging for him."

Scott gave the impression, the very comment about feelings for me had made him feel a little tense too. I tried to argue it with Relik, that Scott really understood just how we both felt about each other. That with everything we have been through together we really had to take this kind offer up from him.

But Relik was still having none of it, he said too many people had died or suffered pain as a result of our situation. He refused point blank to knowingly cause anyone else more possible harm. It hit me so hard then, I suddenly had a big reality check and knew in my heart he was right. It was extremely selfish of me to maybe cause poor Scott some extra pain, especially with what I already knew about him. It dawned on me that maybe the dam snails were right all along, this relationship really was impossible.

I felt a deep pain stab intensely into the moral fibers of my being. What could I possibly do? It wasn't like I could just switch off my feelings and not love him anymore. So, it looked like I was just doomed to exist in some fairy tale love story, one that could never be. And that I would probably die a crazy old bitch with loads of cats and no one would care less.

Some anger started to build up within me, nothing was ever fair as usual, and life sucked again. First, I lost Neil, then I go and fall deeply in love with someone who did not even belong in this bloody dimension. At this moment in time I really wished I'd never even heard of Kachinas. I wished instead I was still sitting in my room back home grieving for Neil. As now I felt like I'd gone completely backwards and not forward in life.

Relik looked sadly up at me, as if he shared my pain and knew precisely how I was feeling. He placed his hand on my face gently rubbing it with his fingertips like he often did. My love for him melted my pain away, I knew inside my heart it was still worth it. This was such a rare special love that even if it was to only sometimes last a day, then so be it. I felt angry with myself for even thinking different for a minute. I tried to not focus on the fact he was at in a female body, as I was about to kiss the lips. But then I remembered this was Sion's swap body, I had not recognized it before, as I'd only seen her briefly when she had visited me in the hospital one time.

"Oh, no I just realised this body used to have Sion in it. She has died too. Oh god, how could I have been such a self-centered bitch," I cried.

Relik looked away his eyes teary. "It's not your fault, Gemma. We all knew the risks that we were taking. She was dedicated with helping to try and stop Aluna especially after she'd lost her brother Jaydin. She would have not had it any other way please believe me."

After I wiped away my tears and composed myself, I asked him how long he could stay and when he thought he would be able to return to me? He said he believed it was for the best if he left right now, the police would most likely be doing house searches of the area. He also assumed he would not be permitted to be a swap for another five more human years. His voice carried sincere pain as he said this. I just wanted to hold him tight and not ever let him go.

Looking into his eyes I suddenly remembered my dream. "Relik, I had the most amazing dream last night, I wondered if you have had any dreams too lately," I asked him. But from the surprised look on his face, I could already tell I had my answer.

"How! How was that possible?" he asked.

"It was a gift from an Ion, when I refused others to suffer for us."

Relik smiled. "It felt so amazing, Gemma, I'm so glad it was sort of real." He said stroking my flushed, smiling cheeks.

Gran gave him some of the special herb tea from the Gnomes to help heal the body he was in. He drank it down fast his face showing the look of, oh god this is just horrid.

After he was finished, I knew he had to go. He held me again in his arms, lightly kissing my forehead and looking deeply into my sad eyes. "I love you and as with each season and year that passes, it will grow even more stronger. You are always carried within me here inside. I promise you, we will spend some more time together again." He let me go and slowly left through the front door.

I didn't cry I knew if I did, I'd feel like I was dying. The pain would just overwhelm my poor soul in a pit of never-ending darkness and it would most likely kill me this time. No, I was determined to make something of my life as I owed it to him and to my parents and not forgetting Gran. I was going to be strong here I needed to toughen right up, I could do this. I was determined I would wait till the very end of my life, if that is what it took to be with him again. But I had a plan, one I had been thinking about recently, one that I felt would be good for everyone involved.

Chapter Twenty-four

Scott came often round to still see me. We remained close friends over the years. I gave him a total make over got his hair cut a bit shorter in a soft, but still manly style. Got him to shave off the goatee and dressed him in, well a smarter but casual sort of look. He seemed to like it, but more importantly so did the girls. I knew though that deep down he still carried a torch for me, but as much as I felt a little something for him too, it was something I could not ever act on. Relik was the one and only love in my life.

Time went so slowly by, or at least it felt that way to me. I had gone back home and Mum and Dad were so impressed with how well and adjusted I'd become. My studies were going good. Everything was going great, apart from the fact I missed him so bad every single minute of the day. I lay there often at night, thinking about if he missed me as much or had he forgotten all about me by now. Time was different where he was, so it worried me that he may feel it was for the best we remained apart.

The day came when I finally graduated from medical school, four years of studying had really paid off. But I had put my heart and soul into nothing else, to keep me strong from pining too much for Relik. Mum and Dad looked so proud at my graduation and Gran and Uncle Rob had come down to see me too. I planned on returning to Gran's place for a while, as I now had a break before I started as a student doctor. I was worried about her too as she looked frailer recently and a little on the pale side. I felt like it was my turn now to take care of her for a while.

Back at Gran's, I felt so at home like the place seemed to envelope me in a harmony of warmth and peace. Gran said it was because of some extra help she was receiving, from another source of the supernatural. Sounded interesting and I agreed it was certainly working wonders. I asked her what it was that was doing this? She replied smiling, "Oh, just a Viking from another dimension."

I frowned. "Oh okay, do tell me more."

"Well, I have been feeling a bit under the weather and tired lately, so I asked for any help making me feel more like my normal old self. I then fell asleep in my chair like I always normally do. Next thing I can remember is my eyes half opening and through tiredness and blurry eyes, seeing this tall blonde-haired man. He had a long ginger beard and deep blue eyes, wearing a tunic with trousers and a pendant with runes on it. He was standing right next to my chair, he smiled with a smile that reached from one ear to the other. Next, he lent down and gently kissed my cheek. Must say I did blush a little, it is such a long time since a man has given me a kiss." She laughed.

I smiled at her. "So, this Viking, he is giving you some healing or something?" I queried still worried, that she should maybe go see her doctor.

"Oh yes, he has filled the whole house with even more positive and healing energy than what's here normally. Oh, and look at this too." She then pulled out from under her top a beautiful purple stone pendant with runes marked in gold on it. "It's a healing stone and the runes craved into it are for peace and harmony of the spirit." I truly believed it, and I was sure I could feel some extra peace in the air. But to be on the safe side I still insisted she made an appointment with her GP. After a few attempts to brush it off as nothing to worry about, she finally gave up and agreed saying she would make one just for me.

Chapter Twenty-five

One late evening just as I was about to go to bed, something suddenly caught my attention from outside my bedroom window. Small bright tiny yellow lights what looked like hundreds of them, were coming up from out of the garden and rising high up into the night sky. I rushed downstairs to get a better look. To my surprise my gran was still up, she was standing outside the back door. She turned and looked at me smiling. "Ah, Gemma. I'm so glad you're up, you really don't want to miss this. I was going to come and see if you were still awake. This only happens about every hundred years or so," she said taking me quickly by the hand and leading me out into the garden.

"What's going on, Gran." I asked.

"It is a gathering of the nature sprites, it's when all the ones that have taken up abode in this dimension go back to their own realm for a little while. They come here from all over the country. Then when they are all finally here together, they fly off to Stonehenge."

"Oh why, what's there, Gran?"

"Stonehenge, it is the portal for their dimension and the main meeting place for the enlightened circle council. Stonehenge is on the most powerful ever lay-line there is," Gran replied as she looked up at the sky watching them all.

"Are they the ones who are responsible for building Stonehenge then?" I queried.

"Oh no, Gemma, giant, mystical beings that used to live in our dimension long ago built it, just before they all left here to go to other realms along with the dragons and Unicorns."

So that is the whole mystery to Stonehenge then. I thought to myself "Wow." I said looking up at what looked like a stream of twinkling glitter streaking up into the night sky.

We watched for longer till it looked like they had finally left and then we both went back inside.

I spent the next few days just chilling and enjoying sitting out in the garden with my gran, chatting about good old times. Things that I'd got up to as a little girl. We laughed about a lot of the mishaps that I'd often got myself into. We were outside one day slipping down some fresh, homegrown, lemonade, and Gran laughed saying did I remember the flies Bill and Bob?

I smiled back saying funnily enough, yes, I did. When I was around six years old, I was terrified of flies. One time I had come flying out of Gran's living room because of two buzzing around the light shade. Gran after comforting me took me back to where they were. She told me not to be scared as these were her friends and would never harm me. She then put her hand out and asked the flies to come and see her. To my surprise, they both suddenly landed right in the palm of her hand. Smiling she told me that their names were Bill and Bob. From that day on I was never scared of flies and in fact every time I visited Gran's place, I especially went and looked for Bill and Bob. Strangely, there always seemed to be two flies buzzing around whenever I would look for them.

"I smiled. What were the flies then, Gran? Some magical bugs."

"They were genies actually and had helped your uncle. He was the one who brought them home."

I laugh. "Umm genies, like a genie in a lamp?"

"Yeah hold on a sec." She goes back inside and comes back with a small, silver, old style looking lamp. She places it on the outdoor table. I pick it up and look at it. Smiling I rub it and out pop two bluebottle flies. I gasp feeling stunned as they buzz around the table.

"They are still here after all this time?"

She grinned. "Of course, my darling, they love it here. Everybody loves it here."

"But err… Do they grant wishes?"

"Yes, but only one per person and can be nothing to do with fate, love, or death. So, no sadly you cannot wish for Relik to return sooner than he is meant to be or anything like that."

"That don't leave you much to wish for, then does it?" I grin.

"You would be surprised."

She smiled. "Go on then rub the lamp once and make a wish. But try and make it good one."

"Umm what did you wish for?"

"Oh, I wished for a never-ending herb garden of all the herbs you could ever think of."

"Oh, good wish there, Gran." I paused. "This is harder than I thought." Suddenly it came to me. "I know, Gran, I know what to wish for."

"Well go on then rub that lamp and say it."

I took hold of the lamp and gently rubbed it. The two flies then flew straight inside it. I looked confused at Gran.

"It is what is meant to happen," she giggled. Say your wish quickly, Gemma."

"I want to wish for the woods here to never be cut down or harmed."

Suddenly the lamp shook and green smoke poured out of it and up into the sky. I got up from my chair and watched it as it drifted off in the direction we took by car to the woods.

"Amazing wish, Gemma, why did I not think of that myself. Once the   green smoke reaches the woods then the wish will be complete."

Smiling, I sat back down at the table and took another sip of my lemonade.

Gran sat down next to me. "I'm so glad it will be safe from mankind, too many trees have suffered because of us."

"I do agree." I replied smiling

Gran smiled back she   then asked me if I still remembered the little old nail lady. I looked confused at her, but something about it seemed to ring a bell. Gran then said when I was about three or four, I'd told her all about the little nail lady. The little lady was an iron nail that lived on the big mirror over Gran's fireplace. Gran had said why didn't the lady show herself to her. I had just shrugged my shoulders.

I followed Gran now back inside to the living room. There she pointed to a small nail that was sticking out of the top of the frame around the large mirror. I looked closely at it, it did not seem to be anything other than a normal sort of nail. Gran said I had told her that while I played alone here in the living room, this little nail would change into a tiny lady wearing a strange orange hat. That the lady would then walk up and down the top of the mirror frame sometimes waving at me, other times talking to me.

"What would it say to me?" I asked Gran laughing.

"Anything and everything, from how you were? What you were playing? And whether you knew the way to Jamaica," Gran replied laughing now too.

"What? Why Jamaica?" I asked surprised.

"Well it turned out she was a witch from Jamaica, she had been trapped in the iron nail by another witch, who she'd fallen out with all because of a man they both loved. Iron you see has some very strong mystical properties and is often used in magic. So then with her trapped inside this nail, it got nailed into the frame of this mirror that was made in Jamaica. It took her eighteen years alone, just to push herself trapped in the nail up and sticking out the wooden frame. I'd bought the mirror about twenty years ago from the market and for a bargain too." Gran smiled.

"What happened to her, is she still trapped in there?" I asked looking up at the nail.

"Oh no, after you kept persisting this little lady was annoying you when you were playing, I decided to check it out for myself. I once secretly watched you when you were in here alone playing. Low and behold I witnessed this little lady walking up and down the frame and whispering to you. After you had later gone to bed, I confronted the nail and asked it why it had not revealed itself to me. After a moment or two she changed again from a nail into the lady and said that it was out of fear of who she could trust. She also did not want to scare the living daylights out of some poor old person. She said some little children are just much more open minded and less scared of things like that. Luckily, I managed with some friends help to set her free and she got transported immediately back to Jamaica," Gran said as she too now looked up at the little nail still sticking out of the wooden frame.

I started laughing saying it was a funny story, but it did sound hard to believe.

Gran said, "Okay, my dear, wait a minute and I'll prove it."

I wondered what she was going to do as she left and went into the dining room. After a few minutes, she returned with a what looked like a picture in her hand. She handed it to me. Looking at it I saw an old Jamaican woman smiling. On the back of the photo was an address in Jamaica and a message, it read:

Words cannot begin to describe how very grateful I am to you and little Gemma for freeing me. Please tell her all about me when she grows up and I see such good things for her future. If you or her ever need anything please let me know. Love Tanesa.

"Wow, Gran that is amazing. When I do close my eyes, I can vaguely remember something with me looking up at the mirror and wishing she would just stop trying to talk to me while I was playing," I said as I handed Gran back the picture.

"You keep the photo if you like, Gemma, you never know too you may need her help one day," Gran said patting my shoulder.

A few more days passed, I called out for my gran and heard her out in the back garden. I went out to find her, she called over to me standing next to an apple tree. As I reached her she said there had been another arrival of something unworldly that I was unaware of. Something magical and an honor to have in your garden. I was excited to see what it would be. Gran took me further to the back of the garden where there was a flower bed of bright yellow daffodils growing. Gran whispered to me I needed to be very quiet now. She slowly kneeled next to what looked like a daffodil, but it was much larger than all the others and had not yet opened. She gestured for me to come up closer, so I kneeled beside her. "I don't think it will be very long, till it's born," she said excitely.

I whispered, "What is it?"

"It is a flower pixie a new baby one, about ready to come into the world. The snails told me just before they left, to expect its arrival very soon." She smiled.

"So, it is born from a daffodil then?"

"Oh, no, not just any old daffodil, the seed of the union between two flower pixies. They choose somewhere special and safe to plant their offspring. Luckily two choose here in my own garden." Gran grinned.

"Where are its parents now?" I asked.

"Oh, they are dead or if you like their essence has joined back with nature. They die right after they plant their child," she told me.

"Oh, that's so sad. It never knows its parents or anything," I replied.

"It does know them, Gemma, don't you fear. As it contains all its parent's memories and knows other things that no other newborn could possibly know. We have species of animals too remember, that play no more part in their offspring's life after birth." She reminded me.

It suddenly reminded me of Relik, not that he was ever far from my thoughts. He had told me how his parents did a similar thing too, although they couldn't have died after, as there is no death in Sanctuary. I told Gran about this. She said that she believed that pixies and Kachinas may be related in a sort of way. There had been some reference to this she heard once down the magical grapevine.

Gran touched the flower head very gently, it suddenly moved. Amazed I watched as the petals slowly started to open. Gran cupped her hands right underneath it, something small and yellow curled up in a tight yellow ball gently fell into her hands. Gran still with her hands cupped showed me and we watched astonished as the curled-up ball opened fully out. It was so cute and beautiful, it was like a tiny sweet child with bright yellow skin and long golden hair and huge blue eyes. It then started fluttering with what looked like tiny white glowing wings. It yawned and smiled so sweetly up at my gran. Gran gently kissed its tiny forehead, just before she suddenly threw it high up into the air. I gasped but didn't need to have worried, as just like a little fledging bird it took flight and zipped fast around the flower bed. We watched it for a while as it investigated the garden and then seemed to disappear. Gran was really chuffed and I was so glad I'd watched such a rewarding experience with her.

Over the next few days I went from feeling quite happy and relaxed, to sorrow again filling up my heart. Being without Relik made me feel almost incomplete as a person. Like half of me was lost or cut in half. I'd not ever believed in soul mates as much as I did now. Gran had an idea, when she had noticed I was having a particular bad day with missing Relik. Four and a half years without any sort of contact from him was taking its toll on my heart and soul. She was not sure if it would work for certain, it had been something she had heard again down the magic grapevine. I told her I would be willing to try anything even if it meant I would only have seconds with Relik. It would be all so worth it. What she told me was, that rainbows acted like telephones to other dimensions. Like they were a Wi-Fi connection for the supernatural world, I just hoped that it had a faster connection than Gran's computer did. But it was incredibly hard to know when one would even appear and how long it would last. Plus, to communicate with Sanctuary, I would have to be standing in a fairy ring at the same time the rainbow appeared.

It sounded like my chances were stacked strong against me and that it may take a miracle to ever work. But of course, I was prepared to give anything a go. After all this was my Relik we were talking about. Gran though had secretly wished, over time I would have got on with my life and forgot about our love. But deep down she truly knew it was never going to happen. She wanted to try and help if possible.

Every day I prayed for bad weather, I'd check the local weather reports repeatedly. I even got Gran to find out if an Indian rain dance could work. She seriously doubted it, as she was unaware of any magic could really affect the weather. But nevertheless, she would try and find out for me. I tried to not be disheartened when the sun shone brightly all day. Every time the weather showed a tiny sign of raining, I'd drive quickly down in my car, just within the speed limits to the woods. But each time I would either get soaking wet without a hint of a rainbow, or it would just be overcast without a single drop falling.

I was beginning to lose all hope of this ever happening.

I had woken up that next morning to the sun shining in all its glory. I got deep into reading a book. As the morning progressed, I noticed the odd black cloud on the horizon. Then half an hour later, I heard the downpour hitting the window pane. Followed quickly after by a crash of thunder and lightning blazing in the darken sky. I was still reading the book, but briefly watched out the living room window as another bright flash lit up the sky. For some strange reason, it made me feel small and powerless, like I was just so insignificant in the world.

I tried to get back into the book, but then I quickly bolted right up and out of the chair as if it was on fire. I flew straight in to the kitchen. "Gran, where the hell are my car keys?" I screamed out loud, as I hunted frantically for them. But before she even had chance to answer, I'd found them under some opened mail on the window sill.

The door slammed hard shut behind me as I made a mad dash for my car. The ten-minute, long ride to the woods felt like hours. I saw the sun peeking its head from out from the dark clouds. I was panicking now I would not make it there in time. Braking hard I jumped out of the car nearly tripping up as I ran. I was trying to keep an eye on the wooded ground, but also looking up at the sky at the same time.

Suddenly there was just a hint of colours in the sky gradually forming, it was getting stronger with each second as I ran. In the hurry, I'd completely forgot where the fairy ring was and frantically looked around. Time was ticking and my hope with each second was fading.

But then a large orange and brown butterfly landed on my shoulder. I looked at it and for reasons I can't explain, I felt as if it was here to help me and followed it as he flew off and further into the woods. It then landed on one of the mushrooms right inside the ring that I needed. I stood in the middle of it, a little out of breath. Suddenly it was there, a magnificent bright rainbow. I shouted out his name at the top of my lungs, repeatedly. Nothing happened, I waited and then tried again. "Relik, please hear me and talk to me please!" I screamed. There was nothing but silence,

Then finally the voice I'd been so desperately longing to hear, spoke! "Gemma, I'm here, I'm here!"

I knew we had to be quick, so even though I wanted to cry, I managed amazingly to compose myself. "Relik, I love you, I miss you so much!" I told him my voice all choked up.

There was an eerie silence. I looked worriedly up at the rainbow, it was still there but getting fainter and fainter. "I love you, so very much too, Gemma," came back his reply just in the nick of time as the rainbow faded away.

It was then I started to cry, but not with tears of sorrow, but out of joy. Joy he did still in fact love me too. I had wished we had longer, but to hear them words was all I needed to keep me going. I looked down at the butterfly and thanked it, its wings opened and closed as maybe in an acknowledgement to me.

I was on cloud nine, as I danced happily through the door to Gran's place. She instantly knew from my reactions it had been successful and hugged me tightly. Now all I needed to do was get through the next five months before he was due to return to me.

Chapter Twenty-six

The date I had written down in my calendar came and went, five years to the day that Relik had returned to Sanctuary. "Why is he not here yet?" I asked my gran crying down the phone to her. She told me maybe there had not been a suitable swap available for him just yet. That I had to remember not enough people, even knew about Kachina's existence. I just had to be a more patient, he will come as soon as he possibly can. She was certain of it. I replied sounding a little annoyed, I had been very patient for five whole years!

It was five years and two months, one week, four days and six hours till I finally got the phone call. The one that felt like I'd just won the lottery or something. I didn't recognize the voice, but just the words that were said, was all I needed to hear. "It's me, Gemma," a man's voice said, as I'd picked the phone up and answered it. I held on so tight to the phone, shaking as I tried to speak.

After a minute I replied laughing and crying at the same time. "Well it's certainly about bloody time." The drive to my gran's place was nerve wracking. I'd played this all out a thousand times in my daydreams, how our reunion would be like. I pulled up outside Gran's place and sat there for a while looking nervously out at the house. Was he really in there waiting for me or was this just yet another lovely dream, like the ones I'd often recently had?

I suddenly saw the net curtain twitch and the outline of a figure peering out through it. I glanced in the car mirror, I was five years older now. What would he think of me? I suddenly started to worry, but then who knows what the body he was in was like. But it did not matter one bit, if it was him, my Relik. He was engraved in my very heart and soul. I was sure I was carved deep inside his essence too.

Turning the front door handle, I slowly walked inside the hall. My heart was pounding out of my chest, my emotions were going into overdrive as I slowly turned the corridor and walked smiling into the living room. The first thing I noticed, was the short bright spiky red hair. Then the fact that he was smaller in height than me. But it was the cute smile, along with his piecing, blue eyes, lighting up his handsome face that made me feel weightless as I drifted across the room. It took me fifty seconds or less, to be snug back in his loving arms.

We talked for hours about what I'd been up to in the time we had spent apart. Relik was so proud of me becoming a student doctor like I'd hoped to. He asked if Scott was still around and I noticed what I thought was a hint of jealously, just in the way he asked along with the fact his body tensed up too. I told him smiling as I kissed him, that we were just good friends. He relaxed and kissed me back.

I cooked everyone a nice meal and we all sat out together in the garden eating it. It was a lovely evening a cool breeze was blowing over us and the smell of Gran's sweet pea plant let off such a sweet aroma. From the looks that we were giving each other, Gran could tell things were getting heated up. She told us both, she had arranged to stay at Uncle Rob's for a few days to give us some quality time alone. I told her she really did not need to do that. Looking at her I was still a bit worried she did not seem like her usual old self. But there was no arguing, her mind was set and that was that. I smiled at her she really was someone very special. I was so lucky to have such a lovely family and never ever wanted to take it for granted. Uncle Rob came over and picked her up in his car not long after the apple pie and custard was served. I noticed Gran had not touched hers so I told her I'd save her some.

Finally, alone we wasted no time, Relik stood up from the chair and then bent down and picked me up in his arms, carrying me up to my bedroom. We started pulling each other's clothes off, but I lost patience trying to get his t-shirt off and gave up as the passion heated up to boiling point.

I cried during and after our passionate lovemaking with tears of joy. For someone who had never made love like a human before Relik was amazing at it. After we lay there holding each other till we finally fell asleep.

Over the next few days we hardy left the bedroom, if we still had clothes on, they never remained on for long. We enjoyed long lovely walks together on the beautiful beach, not far from Gran's place. Relik commented once on its beauty, but I said it did not compare to the beach of transition. He smiled at me and kissed me gently, but that followed quickly with a deep need that ended with us making love right there on the warm sand. I asked him what was better this coming together, or our shared dream one. He replied smiling looking into my eyes this kind for sure.

But then the day came that Gran was returning home, so we needed to tone it down somewhat, even though we both knew that would be extremely difficult. We could hardly keep our hands off each other and wanted to spend as much time as we could together. I went down to make breakfast, when I remembered that Scott was coming over this morning, he really wanted to see Relik once again. I was not sure though if that was a good idea, but what could I say. Relik did not seem fazed by it, or at least from what it appeared when I had told him. Later when Scott turned up, it was like they were two long lost pals meeting up again. Both were strangely relaxed in each other's company. I had not myself seen Scott for nearly six months, so I was glad to see him too. Though I noticed that he had resorted to some extent, back to his old self, with his heavy mental style making a gradual come back. "So, I see the makeover went a bit south." I laughed.

Scott laughed back giving me a pretend punch on my shoulder. "A leopard never changes its spots, Gemma. I feel much more like me this way." He smiled. I smiled back, as long as he was happy the way he was. Who is anyone to judge a book by its cover. As underneath all the brute sort of look, he was still the sweetest guy you could ever wish to meet.

Uncle Rob brought my gran back home a few hours later. She said she was not feeling too good and wanted to take a little nap. I raised an eyebrow at Uncle Rob, he shrugged but I could somehow tell he knew more than he was letting on. Something in his eyes just gave him away.

It was then I suddenly noticed a snail was sitting on the outside of the kitchen window ledge. It looked like it was trying to get my attention with the way it was strangely bobbing up and down out of its shell. I told Scott and Relik, I needed to use the bathroom quick and instead crept outside. In the garden, I slowly approached the snail, still not a hundred percent sure it was a nature sprite. But it was soon confirmed when it rose up and its tiny mouth started to talk. This never ceased to amaze me, how insane it seemed to be having an actual conversation with a snail. Of all the things, they could have possibly chosen to be, why on earth choose to be a snail. But then who was I to question a creature, who was supposedly a much more superior being. I guessed they must have their reasons.

"We are all preparing to leave here soon. The beings in this garden, don't want to chance the possibility of someone new maybe misusing them with a quest for power for themselves. It could be too dangerous."

Confused I asked her what she meant by that as there was no one new   I was aware of coming here.

"Oh dear, oh dear, she has not told you yet?" It suddenly replied, sounding surprised and alarmed.

"Told me what? And who do you even mean?" I was feeling worried now as my mind was trying desperately to figure out what the hell was going on.

"It's really not my place to reveal such things. You must ask her for yourself. Oh, and please send your gran my sincere apologies, I would never have dreamed of saying anything unless I thought for sure you already knew."

Before I could say another word, it shot back into its shell. My feet hardy touched the floor as I raced inside, flying straight up the stairs to my gran's bedroom. I forcefully flung the door wide open. "Gran, what the hell is going on? Don't you dare even try and fob me off with there is nothing. The snails are implying to me that you are leaving here. What do they mean by this?" I demanded, feeling my heart beating faster.

Gran studied me as she lay there looking a little pale and all propped up on a load of pillows. After a moment, she sighed. "Them bloody snails, trust them to go and blab their dam big mouths off. I really did not want you to know about it just yet, not with you having some precious time with Relik."

By this point everyone downstairs had heard the commotion of me rushing in like a maniac. I heard Relik call up, "Is everything okay, Gemma?"

I shouted back down. "I'm not sure yet, Relik, as I need to interrogate my gran."

I looked more closely at her. I sensed there was a lot she had not revealed to me. I was starting to put up a mental wall block in my mind. Trying to protect myself from some fears of what was going on here. But the bricks started to painfully be torn down, as the words fell from off her lips. The one word I'd homed in immediately on was cancer! She had mentioned the dreaded C word. Basically, for the past ten months or so, she had been living with a terminal brain tumor. Only my dad, mum and Uncle Rob knew of this. I swallowed hard as I tried to hold back the tears welling up and trying to break out from my sodden eyes. But that was like trying not to breathe, it was impossible after a while.

"Oh, my darling, stop, don't you dare shed any tears for me. It's just a fact of life and nothing to fear. We are the lucky ones, because we know that there is so much more than death alone."

But the flood gates had opened fully up and were drowning my face. She sat up and opened her arms and hugged me, I sobbed hard into her cardigan. Through the blubbering, I said the snails must know it will be soon if they are preparing to leave?

Gran sadly nodded. "Things have been getting a lot worse lately, I had a feeling myself I was drifting closer to the other side. I was finding it harder to hide it from you. In some ways, it helps you now know. I can relax a little bit better."

I sensed Relik was now on the stair's landing, he had overheard some of the conversation. Gran looked at me smiling and said to tell him to come in if he wants to. I called out to him and he walked in, I went and quickly wrapped myself tightly around him. "I'm very sure she will be taken well care off, wherever she goes, Gemma.

She will get extra special treatment with the connection she has with the powers that be. Any human who is a good soul has this awaiting them?" Relik said softly as he caressed my wet face with his hand.

"I know she will, but I'm going to miss her so much," I sniffled, looking sadly back over at her.

Gran asked to see Relik on his own, that was if I didn't mind. She also thought it was a good idea if I went down and spoke with Scott. She was sure that he would be wondering what all the drama was about. I tearily agreed and after Relik had kissed me, I went slowly back downstairs. Gran told Relik to pull up a chair. "I know what you're thinking, Relik, but I can't go, even if it means less pain for a while. I want to try and be here for her, for as long as I possibly can. You see she is very special and I don't mean just to us. She has the gift that I am certain of. I want her to be able to reach her full potential, then maybe one day the snails will return and keep her enlightened on the ways of other dimensions and such things. I am sure it runs in our blood. Probably due to the fact my great, great, grandfather was the result of a union with a Kachina and his mother. So, I think you and she are much more connected than you think."

Relik smiled. "Yes, I was certain of something extra special about her, I was pulled close to her the minute she arrived in Sanctuary. That sort of connection has never been with a Kachina and a soul inside Sanctuary. I have been a guide soul's before and formed close bonds with them. But with her it was so much different."

"Well you go and prove them obnoxious snails wrong, maybe your relationship really is meant to be after all," she said taking his hand in hers.

Meanwhile downstairs, I'd tearfully told Scott everything. He hugged me tight and said that he would be here for me as long as I needed. Uncle Rob apologized to me for not telling me earlier, but Gran had made him sincerely promise her not to. I did not blame him, I just wished that I'd discovered this a little sooner. It sounded like I did not have much time left with her. I was a little angry too with myself for not picking up on her wellbeing better, especially with me being a medical student. Scott left not long after having a quick hug with my gran upstairs. With having Relik still here, he knew I would have plenty of love and support. Though he told me to call him as soon as I needed him. I thanked him as I kissed his cheek, it had been good to see him again just wish the circumstances had been better.

Chapter Twenty-seven

Gran was sorry it had put a big dampener on Relik's stay with me. This was the main reason she had not wanted me to know now. But I assured her she was not to worry about that, all that really mattered was that I could try and help her to feel as comfortable as possible. Being a student doctor was a handy advantage along with some extra magical medicine that the Gnomes could provide. To be honest I told her this was possibly the best time Relik could have been with me, as my much-needed moral support.

She perked up some more after a good dose of the Gnomes' concoction. But I was still painfully reminded by the snails, that her time was drawing close to an end. Especially as more and more of the spiritual beings that inhabited the garden, had already left for the woods. Gran in the meantime, had wanted me to open up more and let my soul become more connected to the spiritual energy in the lay-line. That I needed to concentrate hard on drawing in more positive vibes, to be aware that everything around me had a powerful aura that I could draw strength from. She also warned me I must stay in tune with my consciences on what felt to be a positive influence, opposed to the bad negative ones which coexisted alongside with each other. It all sounded very complicated, but she assured me it would all start to come naturally. I just needed to believe enough in myself and trust the powers that be. She said she truly believed in me. One day I would be able to harness the magic and goodness that was in this place. It too would always end up being with me, whenever I went. She gave me some of her special secret journals that contained a lot of things that would be really helpful, chants, spells and information on certain beings.

One morning, my gran suddenly perked right up and got very excited, she said that Uncle Rob was going to take us for another little trip down to the woods. That there was something special going to happen today, which one of the last snails still here had informed her of. I was really happy she was going to see something else magical before she left us. But I was still worried about her overdoing it. She would not tell me what it was till we got there, as she wanted it to be a surprise.

Easing her gently into the car, I sat at the back with her, Relik sat up front with Uncle Rob. It was early evening now and would not be long till sunset. We parked just outside the wood and Uncle Rob got Gran's wheelchair that the hospital had loaned her, out from the boot. I helped her in to it and wrapped her up with a warm red fleece blanket. Relik asked if he could push her, I nodded and we all set off.

Gran directed us which way to go. She then suddenly said stop over there and excitedly pointed to a collection of large oak trees. As we got closer Gran said she wanted to walk the rest of the way. I was unsure if it was a good idea or not, but she looked at me pleadingly that I could not resist but help her to do it. Taking hold of her gently I eased her up, she felt so frail it almost made me want to cry. She was shaky as we took the few steps towards one of the trees. Clinging onto the tree, Gran told us that we would all need to be very quiet, so not to scare whatever it was that we were here to see. She told us to look into the middle of the circle of great trees, that she believed it would not be long now. We all kept a look out for anything out of the usual.

The sun started to set and as the last rays of the sun shone down on the forest floor, we suddenly caught a quick glimpse of something glimmering. Whatever it was, it was certainly fast as it darted and flittered in and out of the sunbeams. It looked tall, about six or seven foot and had a slight form to it, though it was still too hard at the speed it was going, to tell what it was.

It suddenly stopped right there in the centre, now we could finally get a much better look at it. It was astoundingly beautiful, but kind of like a ghostly figure. It looked female, in the sense that its shape and features were very dainty. It also seemed like it had long strange sort of hair a bit similar to vines, trailing all the way down its back. It was transparent, but also had a glittering silver centre to it.

"Wow, Gran, what is it?" I asked totally amazed.

"It's a tree nymph, Gemma, in its natural form which is non-corporal and cannot live outside a tree for long, but every fifty years, one is granted this form to be able to travel wherever it wants. But it only has from sunrise till sunset, till it must return and become a tree again. I got a tip off from one of the last snails that one would be here. It's very rare to witness such an amazing event."

Gran smiled as she kept on watching, looking intrigued. Relik held tight on to my hand and looked at me, like he thought this was such an honor too. We all kept watching that is till my Uncle Rob stepped on a twig startling the nymph and it quickly disappeared.

"Oh, Rob, for the love of god do you have to be so clumsy. Now what are we going to do?" Gran said sounding annoyed with him.

"I'm so sorry, Mum, but you know what big feet I have," he said trying to apologise.

Relik spoke up, "Don't worry I think I might be able to help here," as he walked slowly out into the centre. "It's okay, tree nymph, we all mean you no harm. The nature sprites told us you would be here. I am not from this realm myself, but from Sanctuary. Please return and take back up your roots here, we just wanted to watch your magical return to the ground."

All was dead quiet in the woods, but then a sound like a little breeze lifting the leaves off the ground below. Relik quickly stepped back to where we were all anxiously looking. It returned and smiled right at us as the most amazing thing then happened. It suddenly seemed to grow gradually in height to about almost fifty feet high. As it did large roots sunk deep hard into the ground, as it slowly transformed into a huge oak tree with branches coming out from all directions. Green buds were forming and opening out into leaves. We were all dumbstruck as we looked up at this astonishing huge tree which now stood right there in the centre. Anyone who now came to the wood, wouldn't be any the wiser it was not just a normal old beautiful tree.

Gran was over the moon, it was something on her bucket list she had always wanted to see. After she gently patted the tree trunk thanking the tree nymph for allowing us to see her. We helped her back into wheelchair and back to the car. Back at Gran's we put her to bed as she seemed exhausted. The next day she was still tired, but she wanted me to carry on with my spiritual learning.

I noticed one day that a snail seemed to be taking a keen interest on how I was doing with opening up my psyche. He had told my gran later he was quite impressed with my progress I was making so far, to the total delight of my gran. But this was like she had been given a special permit meaning she could finally let go. Because she went downhill quickly that evening.

"Gemma, look in the top drawer and you will see a blue box." I did as she asked and brought it to her. She opened it and pulled out the purple stone pendant on a gold chain. "Here you go, sweetheart, this does really help." She passed it to me. It was the rune engraved one that she said the Viking had given her.

"Thank you so much, Gran, I will treasure it always."

Relik took from my hand and gently placed it around my neck. I tried to keep the tears at bay, but one still managed to escape. I quickly brushed it away.

I had dreaded this day along with when Relik had to leave again. Uncle Rob had called my mum and dad and they were on their way over. I tried desperately to remain strong, Relik kept holding me close and comforting me the best he possibly could. I kissed Gran's cheek and told her how much I loved her and how grateful I was for everything she had done for me. Uncle Rob sat with her as I kept an eye out for the car. I prayed my dad would make it in time, as she started to slip away right in front of us. I heard the car pull up outside, I screamed from the bedroom window for them to hurry up. Dad made it to her side just in time taking her hand and kissing her forehead as he said his goodbyes, she opened her eyes briefly before gently letting go and leaving this plain of existence.

I sobbed pitifully into Relik's shoulder for hours, till I had no tears left. But just when I thought I could be okay for a brief time, Relik dropped yet another bombshell. "I have to leave too, Gemma; the rightful owner of this body wants to return back. I had managed to get another day with his body. He had called me back when you were sleeping last night. But this is something I just cannot keep on doing. Or I may get banned from being a swap ever again. They all fear me becoming a stealer back in Sanctuary."

I burst into tears yet again. I briefly remembered how I'd woken up last night and Relik was not sleeping next to me, but thought he'd gone to the bathroom or something. I could not believe how bad the timing the swaps back could be. But there was nothing I could do but just accept it. I had for a brief moment thought about doing another swap myself, but my dad really needed me here. I could not do that to him even if he had still thought I was myself and not a Kachina. Not to mention I also wanted to wait at least another year or more to swap. As it would then split the five-year break between waiting for Relik's return more evenly. So, we painfully said our goodbyes and kissed each other passionately tears flowing freely from us both. After he was gone, still tearful I picked up the phone and called him.

Dad was so contained in his own personal grief, to have paid too much attention to what had been going on with me. He had not even asked who the guy Relik had just been even was. Mum on the other hand was very curious about everything, especially after ear wigging to some of mine and Relik's conversation. The one thing that had really confused the hell out of her, was when she overheard me saying goodbye to him and how I loved him with calling him Relik. This was going to be very hard to explain I'd thought to myself. Especially then as Scott turned up at the house.

Donna had only just arrived, she had tried desperately to get here in time too. But along with problems with her car the traffic had been terrible. After some hugging and crying with everyone, she went and took care of my dad while me and Mum had that much-needed heart to heart. I hoped that after I poured it all out, that she did not have me committed back to a mental hospital.

I decided to reveal everything to her as I really needed her on board with it all. I would need her to be my rock again now instead of Relik, so I could pull myself through all this pain. I had felt bad with keeping her in the dark all these years, like I had some terrible dirty secrets to hide. When the real truth was, everything was so magical and wonderful, I wanted her to share with me the amazing things that existed and to know about the true love me and Relik shared. If this had been under different circumstances, I would have probably laughed at my poor mum's expression after I had told her everything. But this was certainly not a time that I could even manage at least a little smile.

There was silence for quite a while, as Mum tried to register everything I'd just said to her. She almost looked like she was having a personal battle with the common-sense part of the brain and another side that could be more open minded. She finally said it did all really explain a lot. That also she herself had always been more believing in all the stories Gran had told them. But she said whatever I did that I said nothing of all this to my poor old dad. He was far too fragile, especially now. She said she was sad that I'd not felt able to open up to her about everything before now, especially with the pregnancy. But we agreed no more secrets ever, as I hugged her tightly.

Chapter Twenty-eight

Scott stayed with Uncle Rob, after he offered to put him up. I delicately asked Scott, if he would mind at all being called Relik, just around Dad and Donna. He looked a little uncomfortable when agreeing, which made me feel bad asking this of him. Dad seemed confused why the two of us weren't just sharing the same bedroom. But with Donna here, I said she needed to share with me. It was not like anyone wanted to stay in the bed that Gran had just died in. Which made us all weep again.

I tried to sleep but along with hearing poor Dad crying, I couldn't stop thinking about where Gran was now. I could swear that I could feel her presence still here. Then my mind went to Relik and how I so missed him already. What I'd do just to have one more hug with him right now. But then I saw the sweater he'd been wearing yesterday hanging over the chair next to the dressing table. I got out of bed quietly trying not to wake Donna, who had been the lucky one and managed to fall asleep. I picked up the sweater and smelled it. Yes! I thought to myself it still has his scent on it. At least I could smell him, even if it was only the body smell from the last person who he used to be in. It was better than nothing and I managed to drift off for a brief time. When I woke up an hour or two later, I decided to just get up. I made myself a strong black coffee and went out into the garden. It felt strangely empty, like there was something, sadly, really missing. They had all left, the snails, the Gnomes and the merfairies, even the water Jinn had decided to leave too. Then I remembered the flower pixie, as something suddenly caught my attention from the corner of my eye. I walked over to the flower bed and sat down on the little stone wall that surrounded it. I suddenly saw something small and yellow flittering among the flowers. It was still here, it hadn't left like all the others. I smiled at it and took this to be a positive sign.

Next time I saw him, Scott was at the bottom of the garden right next to the pond. I got up and walked slowly over to him, he turned when he saw me smiling and we embraced. "Your round very early?" I said as I let him go.

"I just couldn't sleep, I have a hell of a lot on my mind," he replied his face looking more serious.

"Oh really, what's up Scott? Anything I can help with?" I asked concerned.

He hesitated to say what it was and shifted his weight from one foot to the other. Like he was preparing to reveal something from his heart. Then it all came tumbling out. "If Relik really loved you as much as he claims to, he would never leave you whatever the cost may be. I feel like seriously kicking his arse for leaving you yet again. Especially at a time like this when you need him the most. He does not deserve you, Gemma. Can't you see that you're worth more than this. I wouldn't ever leave you if I was him."

Looking stern at me he cursed. I paused with shock but quickly retaliated. "Well that's just it, Scott, luckily for me you're not him, are you? You never will be either, however much you try!" I said sounding truly offended at this outburst against my beloved Relik.

"You just don't get it, Gemma, do you? I have tried so dam hard but I can't do this anymore. Pretending to be okay with this crazy messed up situation is destroying my soul. As unfortunately I love you and however hard I try not to, my futile feelings just won't bloody go away. Yet I can't have you, because you love someone that you can't be with either. So, the way I see this, is we are both screwed. What now, you wait another five more years for what? Maybe if you're lucky a week or two at the most together. Or worse even a couple of days. You'll be killing yourself by going through this every five years for the rest of your life. Are you seriously that dumb, Gemma, that you can't see things for what they really are?"

"I think you better leave, Scott, before I regrettably say something that damages whatever we have left of our friendship," I said bitterly.

"What bloody friendship?" he exploded. "You call me up that you need me, and I come running like a little lost puppy. Then you use my emotions against me with your loving gazes that you show without even realizing you're doing it. You know you have been close to feeling love for me, as I really am and not as that parasite of a bloody thing Relik. Are you even really sure you really love him and not me!"

There was silence for a moment, we both glared at each other. "You're just a hussy, who leads people on and you think you're too good for anyone but him," he said as he punched a tree with his fist that we were next to.

I stood dumbstruck, unable to think of what to possibly say back. The only thing I did know was he was so wrong, it was Relik I loved and I was a hundred percent sure of that. But I did care a hell of lot for Scott and seeing this pain he was obviously in scratched deep at my heart.

A cool breeze came over me and the flower pixie again caught my attention. I thought I heard a tiny voice, as Scott still glaring at me, walked briskly off throwing a small box to the ground as he went to leave out the garden. Part of me wanted to call him back, and say this was crazy, we were best friends, but I was so mad.

I suddenly heard it again, that little voice. I went over to the flower bed and there standing on the wall was the flower pixie. She gestured for me to come closer to her. I bent down, I could hear something, but it was so tiny I just couldn't make it out. So, I put my hand out towards her and asked if she would be willing to sit in it. She fluttered into my hand and I brought her up closer to my ear. She told me that Scott was being influenced by something really bad.

"What, ya think? I said in a mildly sarcastic tone. "Is it something supernatural, a being maybe that is possibly affecting him?" I asked her.

"Don't you feel all the unnatural negativity surrounding him Gemma?" she asked. I tried to focus just like Gran had taught me to, but without much luck. My grief and the fact Scott had left already was clouding up my judgments. But if the pixie thought so, then I was willing to take her word for it. She said that something evil, had been recently visiting the pond at the back of the garden. A Naiad she thought may have set up permanent residence there, if it felt the conditions were just right. I asked her what it was? She told me that it was a very bad water spirit, that took great pleasure in causing pain and suffering, that it liked nothing more than causing arguments to arise and would feed off the anger and pain it had helped caused.

"Like a Wakacuna?" I replied

"Yes similar, but a lot worse, I believe it can even lead people to kill," she said.

I was shocked and asked her what I should do about it, but she was unsure as one had not been known in these parts for centuries. I thanked her anyway for her help as she left my hand and went back to the flower bed. I then went and picked up the little box Scott had thrown down. I opened it and gasped out loud, it was a beautiful diamond ring.

I couldn't think straight all day my mind was like a minefield, that felt like it could explode at any given minute. I needed to help with the funeral, as dad was in a bad way. But concentrating on anything was mind boggling and made all the worse by the fact that Scott was now missing, or at least Uncle Rob had not seen him all day.

I was getting very worried, I'd called his mobile phone countless times with no answer. I really did not need all this, not after I'd just lost my lovely gran and thought how unfair life was sometimes. I told Uncle Rob about the possible Naiad that was in the pond and that the minute he saw or heard anything about Scott to let me know.

He rang me that evening telling me Scott was back at his place, that he was packing all his stuff to return to London. I ran fast out of the garden gate and down the street to the apartment above the little café, where Uncle Rob lived. There Uncle Rob let me in and I went quickly up the stairs to see him. He didn't look pleased to see me.

"Don't worry I am leaving on the next train," he spat

"No, Scott, you can't leave! You don't understand you're not being yourself. You're under a spell from an evil water spirit. We need to break the spell, I have suffered something similar myself a while ago."

He glared at me. "Whatever you want to tell yourself, Gemma, but you know deep down inside, that everything I said was true!"

Deep down, yes, I knew that parts were true, but also t everything had been greatly over exaggerated by this evil entity.

Scott kept on packing. "I'm serious, Scott, you really need to come with me right now. I need to figure out how to get rid of whatever is affecting you." I looked pleadingly into his big brown eyes.

Uncle Rob interrupted. "Don't worry, Gemma, I have the cure for getting rid of this shite of a demon." I looked at him surprised. "Not sure why the shocked face, Gemma, didn't Gran ever tell you I was a Druid?"

I frowned. "Umm… no strangely enough she never revealed this to me."

Scott who had now packed all his stuff, was not willing to take any notice of what either of us had to say. So… Uncle Rob decided on a different approach as he suddenly lassoed Scott, with what looked like a rope made of thin branches.

Scott with rage showing on his face tried to break free. But the more he did the tighter it seemed to become.

Uncle Rob smiled at him. "It doesn't matter how big or strong you are Scott, you can't fight this. So, stop struggling. It's made with willow branches blessed by the full harvest moon that had to fall on an Allhallows night."

Scott seemed completely powerless to move now.

Uncle Rob then took out a small bottle of green slimly liquid from the inside of his coat pocket.

He apologized to Scott as he then forced his mouth open and got him to drink the foul looking fluid. I asked him what it was as Scott spat and spattered it all over the place. "You'd be best not knowing, Gemma, as it isn't at all pleasant. All I'll say is part of ingredients involves an eel's heart, mouse brain and crushed up earthworms. And they are probably the best parts of it," he replied with a wink.

"Ewe… how sure are you it will even work?" I said worriedly as poor Scott had now turned a bad shade of green.

"Well it should have quite a fast reaction and he will be cured. But as usual we need to get rid of the evil entity to be sure he is free of it forever," Uncle Rob said as he cut the willow branch rope off Scott. He did this with what looked like an ancient old knife with a carved wooden handle.

Scott slumped down on to the floor still looking an interesting colour. I kneeled over him.

I felt concerned for him. "Scott, are you okay?" I quickly grabbed a handful of tissues from the coffee table, wiping off some of the putrid slime dripping from off his chin.

"Apart from wanting to barf my guts up, I'm good I guess," he replied with a smile that made me feel more relaxed already.

"What about them things which have been said between us. Are we okay there too?" I asked still a bit anxious of his reply.

"Yeah, I'm so sorry, Gemma, for all of that, it was well out of order. I knew I was saying all that stuff, but I really didn't mean it. At least not quite like that. But I do love you though," he said looking away from me.

There was an awkward silence. I gulped hard   as I looked at his handsome face. I felt a little guilty that maybe I had led him on unintentionally.

"I know, Scott, you do. And…I love you too, but just not quite in the same way. But you mean so much to me and I really don't want us to ever fall out.   Friends forever, yeah?" I replied gently squeezing   his shoulder. He smiled sort of sweetly at me and then hurled projectile buckets worth of puke all over the floor. Lovely, I thought as I realized he had also soaked my shoe in some unearthly vomit.

Uncle Rob insisted we must go to the pond at the back of Gran's garden. We had important work to do, that could not even wait for me to wash the vile sick off my shoe. At this rate, anyway with the god-awful smell radiating from my shoe and Uncle Rob's carpet. I was going to have a matching pair anyway as I started to gag myself.

At my Grans, Dad was sitting sadly in the garden, we did not want to make him curious with what we were up too. But that was going to be extremely difficult especially with Uncle Rob now dressed like a druid high priest. Also failing to mention, he was holding a huge garden fork, which he delighted in informing us was made from real human bone. It had to have come from a Wicca, that had been buried underneath a chestnut tree for a hundred years and not a day less. Yeah, this was going to be piss easy to pass off as something you would usually be doing on a warm summer evening. Just to top this all off it was the day before my beloved gran's funeral. Not forgetting the last and important part Uncle Rob shared with us, and that he would have to be completely naked and dance to the chant of the spirit of the earth.

I desperately tried to think of a plausible explanation for all this but was at a complete loss. I had to get Mum involved somehow and get her to remove Dad from the garden, along with Donna who was upstairs listening to music on her iPod at whatever cost. I myself would be needing therapy after this, let alone if poor Dad or anyone else was to witness any of this crazy stuff too.

She worked her magic on him and I still don't know how she succeeded with dragging Donna out. But she managed to convince Dad they needed to go and have a nice drink down at the pub, where Mum and Dad had first met each other. That Donna had always wanted to see this pub that they would often talk about. Donna looked utterly confused, she was sure she never cared less to see it. So, I think to get her to go, Mum must have laid some sort of a guilt trip on her about doing it just for her father's benefit. Primarily with everything she had put him through over the years, that she owed him. Or Mum just paid her to go, either way Mum warned me the clock was ticking, she did not think she would be able to keep them there for long.

We set to work quickly the minute the car pulled away. Uncle Rob throwing down his robe on the grass performed the naked ritual, that he said would call forth the Naiad from the pond. I tried hard to keep my eyes only looking in Scott's direction and not on my Uncle's naked butt. I was not sure what the hell to expect but was very surprised nevertheless when a small golden fish suddenly appeared poking its little head out of the water and was ranting away in what appeared to be Latin. Jesus Christ! I thought to myself, just when I'd got use to the idea about talking snails. Now I had a goldfish snarling at us. Uncle Rob said it was cursing at us with chants of its own. He also said appearances could be misleading, as it started to morph into a large hideous fish like man. Uncle Rob then proceeded to chant more and louder and at the same time throw what appeared to be conkers covered in strange druid symbols into the water. The creature started shrieking horrifically as the water began to bubble and boil around it.

"Now, quick, Scott!" Uncle Rob shouted. Scott took the pitchfork and quickly impaled the withering thing straight through its back. Both the guys started forcefully pulling on the handle and pulled it right out from the water. It lay there on the bank fiercely convulsing as it started to turn into what seemed like solid rock. Uncle Rob quickly removed the garden fork and the thing crumbled into a white powder like substance like chalk. Nothing remained of it, other than this mess on the grass. My Uncle Rob put his robe back on much to my relief, as I'd seen enough of his naked butt and other parts to last me a whole lifetime. But before he'd left, he got out a small glass jar and scooped up some of the white stuff saying that it could come in handy one day. He then brushed the remaining heap of powder into the pond. I was so glad it was all over and not a minute too soon as Dad's car had turned back up in the driveway.

Chapter Twenty-nine

The next day was the day, I got to say my final goodbye to my beloved gran. The service had been lovely just how she would have wanted it to be. Dad had frowned at a few people, who had come to pay their last respects in their ceremonial clothes with flowers and twigs in their hair. But after seeing Uncle Rob turn up to the funeral all dressed in his brown heavy robe and holding a staff, nothing really would have surprised him anymore.

The flowers arrangements were so beautiful and as we looked at them after she was laid to rest. I swore I'd seen a snail or two, hiding within a bunch of Shasta daisies.

I shed more tears even more so when Dad spoke of her being an angel, one that the world had not been ready yet for. I felt so sad for Dad then, because there was so much about Gran that he had not fully embraced. He had missed out on some magical things, that they could have both shared together. It was too late now, but maybe over time I would hopefully be able to tell him everything and he would believe it too. Or possibly, I'd be lucky enough to be able to show him something magical myself. I walked slowly off to have some time to gather my thoughts in one of the remembrance gardens.

Scott had followed quickly behind me. After he had caught up with me, he put his huge arms around me and hugged me. I really needed that but wished with all my heart that Relik was here too.

After the wake and everyone had left Gran's place we all sat in the garden. Dad mentioned unexpectedly, something about selling the house. I shot my Uncle Rob a very concerned look as this place really could not fall into the wrong hands, it had been one of my gran's biggest fears. But I needn't have worried as Uncle Rob was already on it. "I want to take it on, Steven, sell my place and give you half of whatever this house is worth. If that is okay with you?" Gran had left everything equally to them both. "Yeah, that sounds fair, Rob. It does make me feel so much better if one of us lived here, she would always go on and on that this place must remain in the family," Dad sadly replied.

I sighed with relief, now maybe some more of the entities in the enlightened circle would hopefully return here. Especially with Uncle Rob as a Druid and me trying to be more spiritually open. Even the snails may one day come back as well I thought to myself.

After a few more days had passed, everyone needed to try and get back to normal. Although without Gran, I could hardly imagine it was ever going to be the same again. I'd had an extended break from being a student doctor, with my gran dying. But I really could not afford to miss any more time. Dad also had to get back to work at his law firm, Donna to her studies to become a biologist. Then there was Uncle Rob to his well Druid whatever things, along with his part time job of caretaker at the local community centre. Mum didn't work anymore, she had retired early as Dad's receptionist due to arthritis in her wrist. But she still helped as a volunteer for the heart foundation charity shop, near to where they both lived.

Then of course not forgetting Scott, him taking this week off from his tattoo shop to be down here with me was so kind of him. I did not deserve such a good friend and really didn't know what I would have done without him.

That reminded me, I needed to return something back to him. I ran up to my bedroom and removed the little box from my drawer. As I turned around I suddenly got the shock of my life. There standing in the doorway, was a tall, blonde haired man, just like the Viking my gran had talked about. The little box I was holding fell straight out of my hand onto the floor, as I stood there frozen to the spot.

He then spoke. "I am so sorry I was not here at the end, but I had to go and attend to other things in my realm. I hope she was not suffering bad when she left?" he said looking sad.

"Err, no she was reasonably comfortable and passed away peacefully," I replied still nervous.

"That's so very good to hear. I'm glad as she was so special, or should I say still is wherever she is now."

"Do you have any idea where she is now?" I asked hopeful.

"I'm afraid I don't, Gemma. Only the higher up deities of the Enlightened circle would know that."

"Do you think I could possibly contact them?" I asked dubiously.

"That would all depend on you, Gemma, if you were deemed worthily enough. You have met some of them already. The nature sprites or the snails if you like."

"Oh, well yeah they have some very high standards. Not sure if I will ever be good enough for them, but hopefully if I get to the level that is required for them I will maybe get to know one day." I said looking optimistic.

"I hope you do too, Gemma. But sorry I must go now, but blessings to you and your family." He suddenly vanished straight into thin air. I picked up the box from off the floor and ran quickly down stairs. Scott was still outside in the garden. He had wondered where I'd got to.

"Are you okay, Gem?"

"Yeah, I am fine, I was just having a conversation with a Viking from another dimension, like you do!" I smiled. Scott frowned, before nodding like that's perfectly normal. "Oh yeah, Scott, there is something that I need to give you back." I replied, placing the little box on to the garden table next to him. I could tell just from his face he felt awkward as he picked it up.

"I don't really want it back, it is not any use to me, Gemma," he said his eyes not looking up at me.

"Oh, you never know, that special someone could be just around the corner."

He rolled his eyes and got up from the chair. "I better go," he said smiling to me as he put the box inside his jacket pocket. But I couldn't let him escape without a hug first and told him to keep in touch. "Take care, Gem, try and stay out of trouble you know where I am if you need me." He smiled.

I was just about to say goodbye, before something caught my eye. It was a little white dove sitting on the fence, it was strangely looking right at me. It slowly flew off across the garden. My stomach felt all knotted up inside, could it be what I thought it was? I looked serious at Scott. "We have to follow that bird." I run out the garden gate in the direction it had flown. Scott caught up with me as I kept on running, I was trying not to take my eye off the bird in the sky.

Scott asked what was going on, I told him I'd tell him when we got there. It flew onto the ledge of a roof and looked down at us as we stopped outside the house. I pondered to myself, what if I was wrong, what if it wasn't what I believed it to be. But I didn't want to take the risk of not finding out.

As we neared the brown front door my fears were confirmed, as I heard a child crying from a bedroom window that was slightly open. A nasty male voice was shouting at what sounded like a little kid. Quickly facing Scott, I starred into his eyes. "I need you to trust me, you need to break down this door as the child in there is going to die if we don't!"

Scott didn't need telling twice as he started kicking and throwing himself hard against the door. In a few moments, he'd broken right through the wooden door. We pushed some broken pieces of wood out the way and quickly got inside. It was times like these I was so glad

Scott was such a hulking size. In the house a man holding what looked like a belt, came running down the stairs. He demanded to know what the hell we thought we were doing. But before he could say another word, Scott had him pinned by his neck up against the wall. "Scumbag! where the hell is the kid and it better still be okay, or you're going to be six-foot under by the time I'm finished with you." Scott glared into the shocked man's eyes.

I didn't wait around to hear any reply, I just pushed past and legged it up the stairs. In a small bedroom I found him, he was lying in a small heap on the cold wooden floor. He was making a small whimpering sound. He was just a tiny soul maybe three or four years old. I sat next to him on the floor. His blonde, curly locks were partly smothered in blood from a bloodied nose. His face looked swollen and bruised. Scott bellowed from downstairs. "Is the child okay?"

"He's in a bad way, but I think so. We need to get him out and some help."

I placed my hand on the poor mite's back, he cried a little louder.

Suddenly I heard a loud scream come from downstairs. "Scott, what the hell is going on?"

"Not much, Gem, just broke the guy's arm, but I have only just begun."

"Oh, okay… yeah don't hold back."

"I have no intentions of." Came back almost a laugh as I heard what sounded like furniture breaking and the guy asking for mercy.

I softly spoke to the boy. "It's okay, sweetheart, we are here to help you and I am nearly a doctor. I need you to tell me where it hurts."

He cried, "Everywhere."

I lifted his superhero pajama top; his back was covered in fresh and maybe old bruises. I wanted to cry but held it together for him. That was it, I needed to get him to hospital. Slowly I picked him up, he was soaking wet with what smelled like urine. I could not help but shed a tear with how light and skinny he was.

Scott seeing me bring down the poor child, quickly turned and faced the worried looking guy. Scott's face was full of repulsion. Scott waited till I'd got safely out the house with the child to finish dishing out his justice. I ran with the boy to a neighbour pounding hard on the door. An old lady opened the door and looked horrified. The police and ambulance turned up soon. After checking him to my relief, he would survive. The police then brought the man out, he looked like he'd got hit by a train. The guy was ranting and raving he wanted to press charges against Scott for assault. But the police agreed with Scott, that the man should have been much more careful on them stairs, as falling down them by accident could be very dangerous. They then threw him hard into the back of van him screaming, "My broken arm."

I had an officer take my statement and was asked how we knew what was going on. I paused for thought, the truth would be a bit farfetched. So, I said we'd heard the poor child crying and the guy shouting, as we passed by the house. That we just acted on our gut instincts. The officer said it was lucky for the little boy, he must have a guardian angel watching out for him. I agreed as I looked up at the little white dove still sitting on the ledge.

Scott gave me a much-needed hug, as we walked back to Gran's place. I told him everything about how I knew what the dove really was. I said what was scary, was if I hadn't known this information the child would be dead. Scott replied with it must be fate then. He believed everything happens for a reason. Also, that knowledge of my time in Sanctuary was a real blessing. Even though he too had spent some time in Sanctuary, he was unaware of this information.

I noticed Scott's hand looked a little messed up and asked him if it hurt. "No, it's not too bad, anyhow it was worth it. I'd do again it in a heartbeat. Although I really wanted to kill the son of a bitch," he replied looking angry.

I kissed his cheek, "You're the best ya know that?" I said as we walked up to the garden gate.

He smiled before grabbing his bag off the path. "I really better get going, Gem, but remember call me anytime." He winked at me as he walked slowly off down the road.

I went back inside the house, still thinking about what had happened. I wondered if the child had a Kachina inside when I had helped save it, or maybe the Seraph just knew I would try and do something before it had gone and got one from Sanctuary. I guessed I'd never know, but either way was so happy to have been able to help.

Looking at my watch, I thought to myself I better get a move on too. So, I went up to the bedroom and got all my stuff packed and loaded into the boot of my car. I shared some goodbyes and hugs with everyone, before taking one last moment in the garden saying a personal goodbye to my gran. Wherever she was, I was sure she would try and be here too if she could. Part of me sensed this as the case, especially as a strong smell of her perfume she always wore came right over me. "I love you, Gran," I whispered out loud, my voice choked as I held the pendant around my neck now in my hand.

Chapter Thirty

Back at the hospital, I went full force with doing my best. The plan I had thought of, was looking like a real possibility. I'd asked to study as physiatrist after my interim was finished. I had been accepted by a good mentor in this field, not that I was planning on staying in that department as I had my heart set on being a pediatric doctor in the future. But for the plan I had come up with to work, I was needing to be working in the mental health sector. My plan was to find someone, who was so desperate to get out this life for good. That instead of them killing themselves, they could live the rest of their life till just before death in Sanctuary. So, I was looking for someone fitting this profile who would be an ideal candidate. But first I wanted to go back to Sanctuary, it had been about seven and a half years since I was last there. I was confidant I would be allowed back now.

On the beach of transition, it was Valla who appeared to me. I was a little surprised to see her again, but she wanted to apologize in person for what she put me through with the pregnancy. I told her it was a very rough time, but not to fear I already forgave her. She thanked me and smiled, but her smile soon turned to an expression of sadness. She told me no Kachina was permitted to be a swap with me ever again.

I cried and pleaded to know why? She said, since everything with Aluna, the elders had decided to try and not chance anything. I was too strong a risk I would not want to return. To remain here instead with Relik. I tried to convince her after everything which had happened, it would not ever be my intention. I had my family to consider too and had learnt that from my first stay here.

She said she was so sorry, but this decision had been taken away from her and there was nothing she could do.

"Could I at least see Relik for a moment," I asked hopeful.

"Sorry, Gemma, they won't let him. He wanted to be the one who told you himself, but the elders felt it would be far too mentally damaging to you both."

"This is more mentally damaging to me, not being able to see him. How can they be so cruel!"

"Again I'm so sorry, Gemma, I wish there was something I could do."

"Will you at least please tell him, I love and miss him?" I asked tears running down my cheeks.

"Of course, I will." She paused... "Sorry, Gemma, but I must go now."

With that I appeared back in the fairy ring. I sat on the grass and sobbed. All I had wanted was a little time with him. But now I was left knowing this option had been cruelly taken away from us, it was heartbreaking. Instead I would have to carry on looking for a suicidal individual to hopefully fulfill my dreams of us being together. In the meantime, I kept on ticking off the days on my calendar. Waiting for him to return here in a couple of years.

Chapter Thirty-one

The years went painfully by, sometimes I coped well, but other times I felt myself sinking deep down into the ground. I decided to visit Gran's old place again when it got hard to bear. I stayed for a few weeks and practiced hard everything Gran had taught me. A few of the snails even returned and were more and more by the day, willing to spend some time with me.

They told me that Uncle Rob too   was very well entuned with his spirituality. They had been considering inviting him into the Enlightened circle. But with the naked garden rituals he was often participating in with a local coven was becoming less spiritual and more like a sex orgy, involving a lot of bizarre bondage. Ewe... that was not something I wanted to hear as I tried frantically to block out mental images of any of this. Sometimes I really wished the snails would have a little more discretion. Though I did suspect they had a very warped sense of humour, as after revealing this lovely information to me, I'd swear one of them was rolling around in its shell pissing itself of muffled laughter.

I returned back to work and again just tried to keep busy. Time was growing closer; I began to allow myself to become more excited that I would see him again soon. One morning I was in a little coffee shop, two days before

I had calculated his return. I was engrossed in some celebrity magazine sipping down my hot cappuccino, when from completely out of the blue, I felt compelled to look out of the large shop window from where I was sitting. Across the road, I noticed a man standing looking over in my direction. I felt a strange sensation run down the back of my spine and my stomach do a flip. Could it be, was it him? I sat transfixed looking at him, he was still rooted to the spot his eyes fixed on me.

After I pulled myself together, I slowly started to get up from out of the chair. But as I did, the tall, bald guy I suspected was him made a run for it. Shocked I ran outside the shop and watched as he ran off down the street, till I could no longer see him in the crowds. Maybe it wasn't him, I thought to myself. But my heart was telling me differently.

I got home and waited, even watching the clock ticking down the time. Waiting again for the call to come though, just like last time. He had been months late then. But something in my gut knew he was already here and my mind went back to the strange guy from before.

I took some rubbish outside to the wheelie bin, as I did I felt again like he was nearby. Scanning the street which by now was a little dark, I saw a dark figure by the wall at the corner of the road. It did look like it could be the same bald tall guy from earlier near the coffee shop. Dumping the rubbish in the bin, I started walking over in his direction. He stood there looking at me, the closer I got to him the surer I was it was Relik. I broke out in a huge smile as I approached him, but there was something amiss, his expression didn't look pleased to see me. If anything, he looked sad.

Suddenly he spoke. "Please, Gemma, don't come any closer."

I stopped dead in my tracks looking confused at him. "Why, Relik, what's wrong?"

"We can't do this anymore we can't be together anymore. This has to end."

I felt like I was having a panic attack, what was going on? Why on earth would he say something like this? My legs were like jelly and my heart was beating so fast. "Please, Relik, don't say that, you know you don't really mean it." I blubbered.

"Gemma, I beg you not to make this more difficult than it already is. I have realized this is not right for you, or me. You deserve so much better, someone who can always be with you. Maybe even have a family together. Sanctuary is laying down the law as you already know. I refuse to return back ever again."

Grief consumed me, I started to weep as if it came from my very soul. I could tell nothing I could say would get him to change his mind. He looked like he was trying hard to hold his emotions deep within. But I could see him physical shake and I felt my heart split into a million pieces as I carried on crying.

"Please don't cry, Gemma, I do still love you with all my being and I always will do. I will never forget you and who knows one day we may meet again," he said as he cried too. I just wanted to hold him just one last time, but as I tried to approach him he painfully backed away from me. Turning his back on me with his head bowed he mumbled, "Goodbye, Gemma."

He started to walk further away from me. I watched with such sorrow as he disappeared around the corner. I fell to my knees clutching hard at my chest as I couldn't breathe. I thought I was going to be sick as I coughed and spattered with tears streaming down my hot cheeks. I suddenly thought, oh my god my plan. I didn't tell him about my plan. Maybe he would have felt different if I had told him it. I wiped my tear stained face with my hand as I got back up. I then started to run around the corner. I saw a few teenagers and an old man, but no sign of Relik anywhere. I ran to the end of that street, now shouting out his name. Turning quickly into another street, I prayed I would see him. But nothing the street was completely empty apart from a large white cat sitting in the middle of the path. Unknown to me Relik had ran as fast as he possibly could, till he could run no more. Along the way, he rammed himself hard into every passing lamppost, trying to cause himself some physical pain. Then when he had stopped and caught his breath, he wanted to suffer more pain, so he thrust his hand straight through the glass window of a parked car. He'd screamed out in agony as the glass seared through his flesh. I kept on walking and walking till the early hours of the morning, but deep down I knew I'd never see him again.

I myself had no memory at all of how I found myself sitting back in my living room. I would have been there forever not knowing what planet I was still on, if it had not been for the phone ringing and hearing his voice.

Chapter Thirty-two

His voice was a welcomed comfort, but it seemed strange he would suddenly call me at this very moment. We normally talked or met up every few weeks. But I'd only spoke to him the other day. The first thing he said was, "Gemma, are you okay?" in a tone which sounded like he already knew what had happened. I stammered saying something or other, that I just wanted to die. To which he replied sounding upset sit still, I will be there in an hour or so, getting me to promise him I wouldn't do anything stupid.

I kept to my word, as I sat in a traumatized daze. That hour felt like minutes as I heard someone knocking loudly on the door. I felt frozen like I couldn't move and the knocking on the door just kept on getting more and more frantic. Suddenly it sounded like someone had broken down the door. It turned out Scott not getting a reply kicked my door in. He rushed into the living room his face panic stricken. "Gemma, Jesus Christ you bloody scared me half to death!" He grabbed hold of me hugging me tight. After he finally let me go, I asked how? How did he know I needed help? His reply shocked me. He told me Relik had phoned him and told Scott our relationship was over that it could no longer be.

I started to weep uncontrollably, soaking Scott's t-shirt with my heartbroken tears. Scott held me close to his chest as he gently stroked my back. After I had finally calmed down, we sat and talked and told him everything that had happened. He was sorry for the pain I was in and wished there was something he could do to help ease my suffering. I was just so glad he was here.

He stayed with me for a few weeks, making sure that I had lots of well needed TLC. We would talk for hours and he would try his hardest to cheer me up. This place I lived in was a small one bed house, although it was small it was homely, and it was only a five-minute drive from the hospital where I worked, so it was perfect for what I needed.

The garden was nothing compared to Gran's place, but I tried to put some magical elements into it. In the middle I had a small grey stoned water fountain with a mermaid sitting on some rocks. I'd sit for hours reading on a wooden bench, which was covered by climbing pink roses and ivy. Running against the fence I had an array of red and yellow tulips along with a small green and blue clay gnome, poking his head out pushing his little wheelbarrow full of colourful stones. Going along at the top of the fence was a washing line cord, it was full of tea lights hanging in purple and pink painted glass jars I'd made myself. When they were lit on warm summer evenings they looked quite enchanting. There was a reasonable patch of grass where you could lie and sunbathe if you wanted. This was where Scott now stood.

I'd seen him from out of my living room window and wondered what he was doing, so I went out to investigate. He smiled when he saw me, but quickly went back to concentrating. I watched as he gracefully moved his body, it looked like some form of martial arts. After he stopped he informed me it was Tai chi.

"Oh, how long have you known how to do that?" I asked him.

"Strangely from Relik, He learnt it from his host body Russell I believe."

"But why would you have any memories from when Relik was Russell?" I said confused.

"Relik shared with me all memories of anything to do with you. Maybe he thought it might help in some way, I guess?"

"Wow, that's amazing, I never realized a Kachina would be able to pick up so much. And then also be able to pass it on to someone else."

We sat on the bench together for a while. I lit the tea lights as it was getting late and we talked for hours about this and that. I knew Scott didn't have any family left, but normally he was never willing to talk about it. Though tonight he seemed to want to open up. He told me he'd been adopted at the age of two after his teenaged mother had gone off the rails mainly due to drug abuse. His adoptive parents had been great and most of his childhood and early teens had mostly good memories. But sadly, his dad died falling from scaffolding at work when he was fourteen and then his mum died of cancer when he was seventeen. He had no other family he knew of left apart from his grandmother, his adopted mum's mother, but she was in her nineties and lived in Ireland. I felt so bad for him; there was a lot about him I still didn't know.

"I'm so sorry, Scott, it must have been really hard? I can't imagine not having my family around me."

"Don't worry, Gem. It's how it is, no one's fault just life. Sadly, these things happen, there's nothing you can do but just keep pushing through the bad stuff."

His jaw tightened, and he tensed up. Noticing his discomfort, I suggested he could teach me some of them Tai chi moves. So under the moonlight he taught me and we both relaxed.

While Scott had been staying here he'd slept on the sofa in the living room, one night I'd got up unable to sleep and made myself some warm milk. Scott had heard me in the kitchen and came to see if I was okay. "I thought I heard something, are you alright?" He asked wearily.

"I couldn't sleep, sorry I didn't mean to wake you,"

"Oh, don't worry about it, Gem, I was tossing and turning myself," Scott said as he rubbed his shoulder.

"Is the sofa uncomfortable?" I asked as I found myself rubbing his shoulder for him. We shared a special moment as we looked at each other, next thing I knew we were locking lips and sharing a passionate kiss. But I soon pulled away. What was I bloody doing I thought madly to myself. But Scott took me by my waist and pulled me fast to him kissing me lovingly again. I could feel his lust for me radiating from his muscular body. We started pulling each other's clothes off, in a completely frenzied manor. We got down together on the floor our naked bodies caressing each other. But just before it felt as if he was about to enter me, he stopped. I looked at him curiously at why he had ceased and why he was now standing looking down at me his face all sad.

"Scott what's wrong?" I asked worried I'd somehow turned him off.

"This is just so wrong, Gemma, we are going down the path of no return. You love me as a friend and deep down I know this. I can't do this, you truly love Relik and always will. You're in a vulnerable state at the moment," he replied as he grabbed his jeans from the floor. I looked at him and broke out in tears. He was right, I was just so desperate to feel anything other than this agonizing ache in my soul.

Scott grabbed my bathroom robe and wrapped it around me. Tears ran down my face. "I do you love you, Scott, you're my best friend. You mean the world to me."

"I know you do, Gem, therefore I have a suggestion to your problem." He winked. I looked at him fascinated at what that could be.

"What do you mean, Scott?"

"Well I kind of suggested this once before, but not for such a length of time." He smiled. I still looked confused as I tried to gather what he meant. "Gemma, let Relik use my body. I will remain in Sanctuary till this body is ready to die. I have been hiding a lot from you, I myself have been fighting my own inner demons. I want out of this life and if it wasn't for you, I probably would have already done it too," Scott said as he bent down and took my hand in his. He looked at me, I knew this look by now. It was the one that said, I wished you loved me the way I love you. I thought very hard about what he was offering me and Relik. This was big, very big. My moral conscience was in total overdrive. It was like there was a little devil and angel sitting and fighting it all out on my shoulders. I really wanted to just say yes and not think twice about it again. But that dam angel was whispering to me, this is so wrong. I could not give him an honest answer yet, as this would need some serious consideration. I needed time to dwell over it all, I asked him to give me a week and I would give him my answer. He planted a kiss on my forehead. "One week then." He grinned.

It was decided he would go back home he had some things he needed to take care of. But he kept on repeating, this could be the answer to everyone's problems. After he had gone I was left alone with my thoughts. I so wanted to be with Relik and had been all prepared to get some poor other lost soul to make this happen. But now I was faced with such a tricky dilemma with Scott offering up himself. I felt there was only one place I could go to find the answers to that. Gran's old place!

Chapter Thirty-three

Just being back in the magical garden again, seemed to already make my thoughts be much clearer. This place was like food for the soul. I closed my eyes and called out. Please be willing to talk to me I need your advice I said out loud. They had been all too ready to inform me all about my uncle's unholy antics, so I hoped I could get them to talk when I needed them. So, I waited and waited.

Time ticked by and nothing. I guess I am still unworthy I thought to myself as I got up to leave. But I was taken back by surprise, as a voice clear as day spoke. "You already know the answer you seek, Gemma. You really don't need us to tell you what you should or shouldn't do," said a snail that was sitting on a little garden gnome statue.

I looked down at it feeling annoyed. "Well if I really thought that I wouldn't be here now."

"That is because you humans just don't trust your intuition enough. Allow yourself to listen to what you know you can really live with. If your conscience can be clear and not tormented, then it's the right path you should take. Otherwise you and me both know, you will only regret it till the end of your days."

Oh, you blasted snails, I thought madly to myself. But he was right, completely spot on. I'd bloody drove five hours down here, just to hear what I deep down already knew in my heart.

The next day I returned home. He had waited patiently for a week for my response back. I was certain I knew what my answer was going to be. There was a knock at the door, I opened it and let Scott in. He was obviously nervous, as I repeatedly tried to convince him to sit down. But he kept pacing up and down my living room floor, occasionally glancing over at me. I thought the best thing to do was to just come straight out with it. Taking a deep breath in and then out. I looked straight at him.

"Scott, the answer is no! Umm... I can't live with it. I know this will sound really selfish, but... I still need you too in my life. You're my best friend and you have been there for me always. With everything we have been through together, it would not seem right. The demons you have we will fight them off together. You don't need to feel alone, I will be there for you, just as you have been there for me. Plus no way will Relik ever agree to it anyway."

Scott looked down at the floor. He wiped tears now falling down his face. "I understand Gemma and that means so much you saying all this. I guess you're right about everything and no... he would never agree to it."

I sat down next to him and put my head on his shoulder. He pulled me close and hugged me.

"Though if you ever change your mind, then let's talk. Sometimes we can only keep the demons away for a while till they creep back in." I sighed... "Yeah I know, but we have to keep on fighting. Never give up ok?"

I kissed my forehead. "I will try not too Gemma." I'd thought to myself I'm glad he did not put up a fight that he was not against my decision. He left a few hours later after we had shared a pizza and a glass of wine together. He kissed my cheek lightly as he left through the front door. Though he paused for a moment as he looked back at me.

Another week passed by, I threw myself back into my work. Forgot all about my plan for finding someone for Relik. The whole experience with Scott had made me feel a lot different about everything, along with the painful feelings of being rejected by Relik. I couldn't help thinking to myself, he should have fought much harder for our love, especially with everything I was prepared to go through for us to be together. I felt he had given up on us far too easily, which hurt a lot.

One evening, I decided to give Scott a quick call, I was missing him as I had not heard from him at all last week. I called his number several times throughout the day without any luck. I guessed he must be busy or something, but as the day progressed further I started getting an uneasy thought creep into my mind. One that I couldn't seem to shake off. This unnerving feeling then grew dramatically when I got a call straight out of the blue from my Uncle Rob. The reason he had called was to tell me Scott was at my gran's old place with an important letter for me. I asked my Uncle Rob to get him to talk to me on the phone, but Scott refused to. Getting mad I shouted at Uncle Rob to somehow make him, but he was having none of it and said to pass on the message and that it needed to be this way. I was getting more nervous as he was starting to freak me out. Uncle Rob told me all Scott kept saying, was everything would be explained to me in the letter. I asked Uncle Rob to make sure Scott did not leave Gran's before I got there. Uncle Rob said he would try his best, but Scott was a big lad and he was completely out of blessed willow branches.

Chapter Thirty-four

The long drive down there was unpleasant, I got stuck in traffic, made all the worse by having a hundred bad thoughts floating about in my messed-up brain. There was something amiss with Scott. Had I been so blind and consumed in my own self-pity that I'd failed to really help him. Even though I had said we would fight his problems together.

Stupid, stupid bitch! I cursed to myself as I finally pulled up outside the house. I raced nervously up the little cobbled garden path. The thought of something ever happening to Scott was unbearable. Uncle Rob opened the door before I even got the chance to knock on it. I could tell from the look on his face, I was already too late. "How long has he been gone?" I screamed standing frozen to the spot.

"Fifteen to twenty minutes I'd reckon."

I asked for the letter and he passed me it. I tore the envelope open and started to quickly read. The letter said:

My dearest, sweet Gemma,

First things first, my girl, stop damn panicking right now which I know you will be doing. I am completely fine and am in no danger whatsoever, so get them silly thoughts you're having straight out of your beautiful mind. Secondly, I love you, and Relik is a bloody lucky son of a bitch. Personally, I still don't think he really deserves you, but hey I have accepted it now. And I guess, other than me, of course, he's the best guy for you. I sort of understand where he's coming from with why he did what he did, with refusing to carry on the way things were. It was because he loves you so much and does not want you to suffer any more. I respect him for that. But you know seriously, Romeo and Juliet hold no candle to you and Relik's love story. Flip, if I was planning on sticking around, this whole story would make a best seller if a novel was made of it. But that's just it, Gemma, I'm not actually planning on being here, hopefully. That is… if I can convince your stubborn lover to bloody take up my offer. He can be somewhat pig headed and so unselfish, that it could be a pretty big challenge. But I'm up for a fight, I don't intend on give up trying easy. He needs to realize this will benefit me greatly too. So, as I am sure by now you have guessed the next time you see me, well my body at least, it will hopefully, in fact, be Relik who is inside it. I'm so sorry I have done it this way, but to be honest, we both know it was the only way as you would have never allowed me to. I would have liked a goodbye kiss though, but I will wait till near the end of my life for that. As we will see each other again, even if it's just for a brief time. So, this is goodbye just for now. Don't you dare ever take a single day with him for granted, as this is my gift to you both. Don't forget me either. Love you, Scott xx

I gasped. Before Uncle Rob had the chance to ask what it said. I'd thrown the letter at him and ran as fast as I could get to my car. Scott, Scott! You are such a damn bloody pain in the neck, I thought madly to myself as I started up the car and drove fast to the woods. What though if I was too late? I panicked. But I kept telling myself there was not a chance in hell he would be able to convince Relik to do this. I was certain nothing would get him to ever swap again, especially with Scott. Turning into the layby right near the woods, I jumped swiftly out of the car, running with my heart beating like it was going to explode out of my chest. Part of me started to think what if? What if Relik really went for it? But I couldn't allow myself to think it, as could I live with the fact Scott had sacrificed himself for me? What was with all these guys, who were so willing to give up everything for me? I certainly didn't deserve it that was for sure. I saw the fairy ring now, but it was empty. Did it mean Scott was in Sanctuary trying to convince Relik or what? I had no way of telling other than to wait.

After about three hours of standing around alone in the pitch cold dark, which in these woods was unnerving at the best of times, I started to freak out. I'd heard what sounded like the bloodcurdling screech from a banshee fox. I once heard them before when my gran was still alive, after we had come here once. She had brought me here to learn more about the supernatural things that inhabited this old place. She'd warned me there were some evil bastards out here, who prayed on anything that listened closely enough to their horrid calling. You had to be careful you did not get hypnotized by their inhuman cries. As they would basically make you follow their haunting screams, being drawn further and further into the woods, till finally you were trapped in their lair and never seen alive again. They wanted vengeance against all humans, because of something centuries ago.

Some ancient druids had conjured up a spell to trap them for all eternity in the bodies of foxes. All because they had stolen human babies and eaten them, believing their flesh and souls were uncorrupted and give them more power. The only way you could tell a normal fox from a banshee would be to spray them with saltwater. They hated it and would start to burn from even a small amount of it. I felt frantically inside my bag for the little water pistol I always kept in my purse after my gran had told me about them. Grabbing hold of it I looked nervously on hearing another cry from one which seemed closer now. Something moved in the dense grass and after I finally decided Scott was not here. I legged it fast to my car with the unnerving feeling of something right behind me. I fumbled with my keys on hearing a loud breathing noise getting closer and closer. The hair on the back of my neck rose. After finally getting inside the car I locked the door and started it up, not wanting to be there for a minute longer. Maybe? I thought to myself, Scott had gone to a different fairy ring or something. I made my way back to Gran's house. Quickly inside I threw the car keys on the sofa and flopped hard into a soft armchair. I sat there for a while wondering what to do now? When from the window that backed onto the garden, I suddenly saw something in the darkness move. I stood up and slowly walked over to the window to take a better look. It was a person, it was Scott, but wait it wasn't Scott? Oh, my god it was Relik!

Chapter Thirty-five

The strong bond we shared, always meant I somehow instinctively knew. But I was worried my judgments were clouded, because of everything that had happened. Was my connection with him being over shadowed with me wanting it so bad to really be Relik? I needed to be a hundred percent sure before my heart skipped another beat. I slowly walked into the garden, he stood and faced me. I could already see the tears in his eyes as a smile started to turn up in the corners of his mouth. Being back in his arms felt like heaven, it almost didn't feel real. I was worried I'd wake up and this would all be a dream. But it was real and as we kissed, we cried.

Relik told me how Scott had suddenly appeared in Sanctuary, calling or he should say demanding to see him. He then put his case to him explaining his idea and everything. At first Relik was adamant there would be no way in hell he would ever agree to the swap. But Scott was very persuasive, especially when he told him it was only a matter of time before he was the one who would have your sexy body. Relik said he felt an intense jealously over this. Scott also told him how he needed this swap to happen as much as we did because of what he himself was suffering. He believed he'd end up killing himself otherwise. Scott said no one would ever have your heart but me. That you would barely get through your life in one piece without me. Not to mention Scott, said he would kick my ass, or whatever I had under my wisping tail all the way back to my realm if I did not agree.

That sounded just like Scott, I laughed.

"But Relik, was Sanctuary okay with this situation?"

"No to begin with they weren't, but they feared I would just end up becoming a stealer otherwise. So reluctantly after a lot of consulting they agreed to it. I got them to assure me Scott, would never be put into the mist lands either," Relik replied as he took my hand s looking lovingly into my eyes. I don't think we could ever have been more grateful to Scott, for what he did for us both.

Life together over the years that passed was amazing. I became a pediatric doctor just like I had wanted to be saving a lot of children's lives. We had two beautiful babies together a boy and a girl. Everything went according to plan, just like the tunnel of potential had shown me. It was Relik who was the man with me in my visions all along. Donna got happily married to a good colleague of mine, and life was just peachy. We grew old together and we never took a single day for granted together. Just like Scott had asked me too in his letter. I was after showing I could be trusted to help keep the balance finally accepted into the enlightened circle. Just as my gran had showed me the way, I did the same for my own children and granddaughter Brielle who was named after my beloved gran.

We moved in my gran's place when we both retired and lived happily content there for a good few years. I was cleaning upstairs one day when I felt a sudden pain in my chest. I looked up to see the Viking, the same one I'd seen standing in the doorway so many years ago. I smiled at him but realized something. "Who are you here to help? Me or Relik?" I asked nervously.

"You I'm afraid, Gemma. Your heart is very bad. But I can make the time you have left much more comfortable though," he replied.

I'd thought as much, but this did make me sad. I had wanted to be the one left behind, so that I got to give Scott that goodbye kiss. To say thank you for everything. But if that was the way it was going to be then who was I to argue. Life had worked out well, I couldn't have been happier. Though just when I'd accepted my time was drawing close. Relik suddenly became very ill with pneumonia. The doctors warned me and my children he didn't have long. I cried at his bedside in the hospital as he got closer and closer to death. Holding onto his hand we shared our loving goodbyes, he regretted nothing at all apart from wishing he could take me back with him. I kissed him saying I loved him so much and would for always. That I still believed in my heart, we would somehow see each other again one day. Relik then drifted into a coma and I waited for him.

An hour later I felt a little cool breeze over Relik, then I felt him suddenly leave along with it. A tear ran down my face as Scott's eyes opened. He struggled to breathe but I quickly managed to calm him down by telling him that it was me Gemma, as I smiled at him. He smiled back. "Thank you so much, Scott, for everything, I really don't know how to ever repay you for your kindness to me and Relik?" I told him.

"Oh, yes you do, Gemma, that goodbye kiss, remember?" he said grinning from ear to ear. I lent down and gently kissed his lips tenderly. "Perfect." he smiled, then stopped breathing and he too was gone. It had been so quick, I wished we could have had a little more time together. But this was how it worked. So now with my Relik gone, I was ready to leave this life too. But unfortunately, it took another two long months, for that to happen. I felt myself break free of my body, similar to when I had done the swap with Valla. Though this time there was no connection left with my body. I felt so free and was surrounded by other souls including my lovely parents and beloved gran, my grandfather I had met in the dream and Uncle Rob. But more importantly and so shockingly Relik was here too!

We were all in the seventh dimension also called Heaven. Unknown to me, Relik had secretly been having some enlightenment from the snails. They told him that one of the eight dimensions which existed was where all the dead souls went to. That when he had to leave Scott's body, there was a way of him being transported here instead of back to Sanctuary. That souls and Kachinas weren't so different after all. Though he needed to understand this was a one-way trip. he could never return to Sanctuary. Of course, this suited him perfectly fine as he wanted nothing more than to be with me for the rest of all time.

He had worried it would not work, but the snails kept to their word and made sure he passed over here. "So, we are indebted to them slimly critters?" I laughed.

Relik smiled. "In fact they said they were indebted to us because of what went down with Aluna."

I suddenly heard someone behind us and as I turned I happily saw it was Scott!

The three of us laughed and embraced tenderly. Though someone else, who'd also been a special part of my life and the main reason I'd gone on this path then appeared. It was Neil... I felt so happy but guilty all at the same time. He smiled telling me it was meant to be this way, he couldn't have been happier for me. I smiled, as it had been in life, it was impossible to be anything other than happy in his company.

The End